Rachel made Kane a...

She awakened feelings he'd always kept control of. He felt the heat rising within him as his hands moved over her slimness. Not just the softness of her flesh but the softness within her reached out to him. He wanted to lose himself in her. It didn't matter that he wasn't any good for her. That she deserved much more. He wanted her.

Kane made Rachel want again, feel again.

This attraction hadn't been in her plans. She'd come only to bring him his infant niece. But she couldn't pretend this was simply about baby Heather anymore. That was the problem. Nothing was simple. After fifteen years away, she hadn't banished the thrill when Kane Riley looked at her, touched her. And now that she knew his kiss, knew what being with him and baby Heather felt like, she wasn't sure she could ever forget it....

Dear Reader,

It's the little things that mean so much. In fact, more than once, "little things" have fueled Myrna Temte's Special Edition novels. One of her miniseries evolved from a newspaper article her mother sent her. The idea for her first novel was inspired by something she'd heard a DJ say on her favorite country-western radio station. And Myrna Temte's nineteenth book, *Handprints,* also evolved in an interesting way. A friend received a special Mother's Day present—a picture of her little girl with finger-painted handprints and a sweet poem entitled "Handprints." Once the story was relayed to Myrna, the seed for another romance novel was planted. And the rest, as they say, is history....

There are plenty of special somethings this month. Bestselling author Joan Elliott Pickart delivers *Single with Twins,* the story of a photojournalist who travels the world in search of adventure, only to discover that *family* makes his life complete. In Lisa Jackson's *The McCaffertys: Matt,* the rugged rancher hero feels that law enforcement is no place for a lady—but soon finds himself making a plea for passion....

Don't miss Laurie Paige's *When I See Your Face,* in which a fiercely independent officer is forced to rely on others when she's temporarily blinded in the line of duty. Find out if there will be a *Match Made in Wyoming* in Patricia McLinn's novel, when the hero and heroine find themselves snowbound on a Wyoming ranch! And *The Child She Always Wanted* by Jennifer Mikels tells the touching tale of a baby on the doorstep bringing two people together for a love too great for either to deny.

Asking authors where they get their ideas often proves an impossible question. However, many ideas come from little things that surround us. See what's around you. And if you have an idea for a Special Edition novel, I'd love to hear from you. Enjoy!

Best,
Karen Taylor Richman, Senior Editor

Please address questions and book requests to:
Silhouette Reader Service
U.S.: 3010 Walden Ave., P.O. Box 1325, Buffalo, NY 14269
Canadian: P.O. Box 609, Fort Erie, Ont. L2A 5X3

The Child She Always Wanted

JENNIFER MIKELS

Silhouette®

SPECIAL EDITION™

Published by Silhouette Books

America's Publisher of Contemporary Romance

To Dan,
Always

SILHOUETTE BOOKS

ISBN 0-373-24410-X

THE CHILD SHE ALWAYS WANTED

Visit Silhouette at www.eHarlequin.com

Printed in U.S.A.

JENNIFER MIKELS

is from Chicago, Illinois, but resides now in Phoenix, Arizona, with her husband, two sons and a shepherd-collie. She enjoys reading, sports, antiques, yard sales and long walks. Though she's done technical writing in public relations, she loves writing romances and happy endings.

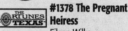

Chapter One

"He doesn't like company. Isn't friendly to anyone."

Rachel Quinn had let Velma Monroe's unasked-for advice float past her. It didn't matter that Kane Riley wouldn't be pleased to have company. She was going to see him.

"He has the *Maggie Lee* now, a cabin cruiser to take out the weekend warrior types," the woman said on a little laugh while she punched in the prices of Rachel's purchases on the lone register at the Grocery Mart, a family-owned grocery store. Velma was pear shaped with a no-nonsense, short hairstyle. A few gray threads wove through the soft-brown color. But despite a stern look, an often disapproving one, she had beautiful brown eyes.

"That's the boat that Charlie Greer named after his late wife."

Rachel recalled that from when she'd lived in Hubbard Bay years ago, and phone calls to Lori Wolken, a close school friend, had helped her play catch-up.

"And he bought himself the *Sea Siren*. It's one of those touring boats to take the summer vacationers on cruises around the islands or for whale watching."

Hunger gnawing at her stomach, Rachel placed two candy bars and a can of soda on the counter.

She watched the woman's eyes shift with a curious glance from her blondish-red hair to the infant in Rachel's arms. "Thought you'd have redder hair. Most Quinns do. You've been gone from Hubbard Bay for some time, haven't you?"

"Sixteen years. I was fifteen years old when my family moved away." Quickly she paid Velma for the items, including the package of diapers and a can of baby formula.

Velma cast another look at Heather. "Young one. Practically newborn, huh?"

"Yes, she is."

"What's her name?"

"Heather," she answered while pushing the cart forward.

Somehow she managed to leave the Grocery Mart without answering Velma's last question. "Why are you back in Maine?"

People would know soon enough. Even when Hubbard Bay's population blossomed with tourists, locals kept close tabs on their own. Why she'd returned would be at the top of tomorrow morning's gossip.

Rachel didn't care. She refastened Heather's car seat. This baby was all that mattered.

She slid behind the steering wheel, then dug in the grocery bag for a candy bar. Before she began driving down Main Street, she'd devoured half the candy. Like so many other streets in town, this one led to the harbor and the piers for the lobster boats, the ferry landing, and the docks for the yachts, sailboats and tour boats.

Nearing the harbor, she rolled down the van window. The smell of the ocean, the sound of a foghorn, the squawk of gulls filled the air. From the crowded parking lot near the pier, Rachel spotted the *Sea Siren* and negotiated a parking space. The sky above the Atlantic carried a gray cast and the promise of a June storm. Summer tourists in windbreakers and funny-looking hats milled around the deck of the boat, chatting and laughing.

She sensed she didn't have a lot of time. Rushing, she unfastened Heather, and with her in her arms, Rachel hurried from the van and across the parking lot to the pier.

In her path a grizzled-looking fisherman dressed in a yellow slicker was carting a bushel of crabs from his boat. Without slowing her pace, Rachel side-stepped him and half ran, half walked along the planks to avoid jarring Heather too much. The sooner she made contact with Kane Riley, the better.

Then she saw him. He looked different, she decided in that instant. More sinewy, with muscled arms and long, sturdy-looking legs. Taller. A man of the sea, with his deep tan. The boy she remembered and had ogled had changed. Handsome features had strengthened. High cheekbones carved into his face with its strong, square jaw. A touch long, shaggy, his dark hair ruffled beneath the wind. "Kane?" She stopped on the pier, waited for him to look up. Straight, dark brows lowered over piercing, smoky-gray eyes as he studied her for a moment—a long moment. She'd forgotten how deciphering those gray eyes were. Feeling weighed and measured, she almost squirmed. "Do you remember me? Rachel Quinn," she yelled to him. "I need to talk to you."

He cast off the bow line. "Don't have time."

"I've traveled more than twelve hundred miles to talk to you." He tossed the stern line onto the dock. "It's really important. Vital," she mumbled to herself as he strode toward the wheelhouse.

Rachel abandoned any notion of trying to shout over the chugging of the engine. Perfect timing, she berated herself. With Heather cuddled close and nowhere to go, she watched the boat, filled with passengers, motor out of the slip. The bow rose, rode a small swell, then lowered. She took a deep breath, drawing in the smell of fish and seaweed. If she'd arrived earlier, she'd have had a chance with him, could have made her announcement.

Well, she hadn't. She ambled back to her van. So she'd have to handle this situation differently. She knew where he lived. He'd inherited Charlie Greer's home, the same house that had at one time belonged to her family. She'd lived there until her teens.

The street his house was on led to the top of a cliff. The cottage was perched at the end of the street, and on a clear day it had a spectacular view of the sea. Odd that fate had brought her back here, that Kane, the one person she needed to see, owned it now.

The white clapboard house with blue trim was weathered from the wind and in need of paint. Wooden steps led to a wide wooden porch. The home, with its steep gable roof, had a full attic, high ceilings, a brick fireplace and plenty of creaky floorboards and groaning doors. A fish-shaped weathervane on the roof spun to point north. Rachel recalled her mother had loved the house, loved being so near the water.

She parked at the curb, facing a sky darkening with a storm. Within an hour, it rolled in from the north. Through the closed windows of her van, the wind howled. In the pewter-colored sky, lightning cracked, splaying fingers toward the choppy-looking water. Waves crashed against the rocky coastline even before rain began pounding.

She shifted on the seat behind the steering wheel, ate a second candy bar and downed a can of soda. Despite the junk food snack, her stomach growled. Heather slept, unaware of the storm. Rachel assumed that Kane had docked hours ago. So where was he?

He wondered what she wanted. Kane had no problem putting a name to her face. He hadn't seen Rachel Quinn in more than a decade, but she'd been the girl he'd gone to sleep thinking about, the girl he'd never asked out, a red-haired beauty with shoulder-length hair, a girl with looks that had promised in time to rock some man's world. Just the sight of her had been a bright light to him during some of the most dismal of days.

Slim, long-legged, about five-five, she wore her hair shorter now, chin length. It swung with the movement of her head. She'd changed a lot, he reflected as he recalled the baby in her arms.

He could only guess why she'd wanted to talk to him. Either she was the sentimental type who'd needed to see the family homestead, or she wanted to find his kid sister. They used to be good friends.

He shrugged and finished his dinner, a meat loaf smothered with brown gravy. A quiet thing, Rachel had always waited outside the house for Marnie. He figured she was afraid of the old man. Ian Riley had been drowning his sorrow in booze nightly and was more often drunk than sober.

Kane cursed himself for not giving her a few minutes earlier. He figured he owed her. Big-time. Sweet, she'd offered his sister friendship when shunning Marnie had been the in thing to do. Kids could be cruel. He hadn't cared that he wore sneakers with holes, but their poorness had proved harder for Marnie. At thirteen, she'd agonized over the thrift-store clothes, over the taunts. His sister's saviors had been Lori Wolken, some other girl and Rachel Quinn.

Looking up, he stared at the window and the rain pounding against it while a waitress poured more coffee in his cup. He'd driven to Bangor earlier. He was in a foul mood, mostly because of the rain. If a downpour lasted for days, he'd lose money.

Living nearby was a certain brunette with no interest in anything but good times, which suited him fine. He kept his life free of complications, of connections with others. He always would.

As nightfall closed in on the town, Rachel grumbled under her breath. This was dumb. While she was sitting in a car, waiting for Kane, her legs cramping, he might be hunched over a warm meal somewhere. Expecting Heather's cry any minute, she yanked the giant denim diaper bag from the floor to the seat and hunted for a bottle of formula that she'd made up in a gas station rest room earlier.

When lightning flashed again, she glanced at the cottage's wide porch. She should have known this wouldn't be easy. Nothing had been going right since she'd left Texas. She'd never believed in omens or superstitions. She'd always been far too practical, too level-headed for mystical ponderings. But she'd had a flat tire in South Carolina, the alternator had quit outside of Washington, D.C., and the water pump had begun to leak at Maine's state line.

Weary, she slouched on the seat, wanted to close her eyes. She might have, but a beam of headlights sliced through the curtain of rain. Rachel squinted through the van windows and the downpour. An old-model black truck maneuvered into the driveway beside the house.

In seconds the truck door opened. Shoulders hunched against the rain, a man raced to the house in several long strides. Wearing a seaman's cap, a yellow slicker, jeans and work boots, he might be anyone. That sounded like a logical reason to her for stalling. In truth, uncertainty plagued her, kept her in the van. Coming here to see him was what she'd promised to do, but was she doing the right thing?

A light went on at the back of the cottage. It was the kitchen. She'd dried dishes often enough at the old porcelain sink. Mentally she geared up for the next moments, considered what she'd say. This situation was too important for her to mess up. But she was no more prepared now than she'd been hours, even days, before, and her empty stomach knotted.

Nerves had kept her from eating more than the candy bars. She could have excused uneasiness to old feelings and memories of when he used to make her teenage heart palpitate. Unbeknown to him, Kane Riley had been the first love of her life. In retrospect, Rachel concluded that she'd fantasized about him because he'd been forbidden fruit, the bad boy. But she wasn't fifteen anymore, innocent and naive; she was experienced, had had a lover. Whatever nervousness was besieging her had more to do with concern for a baby than puppy love.

As she slid out of the van, the wind whipped at her, tossed down her hood. She yanked it up again, then stretched into the back seat to unbuckle Heather from her car seat. She wrapped her snugly in a heavy blanket and nestled her against her chest and beneath the opened rain slicker.

Almost punishingly the rain whipped at the side of her face before she reached the steps. They creaked beneath her feet; memories flooded her. As a child, she used to chase up the stairs after her brother. As a teen, she'd come down those stairs with the gangly sixteen-year-old star of the school basketball team.

On the porch now, she dabbed a hand at her wet face before she knocked on the door. In a matter of minutes she would fulfill a plan that had started in Texas almost two weeks ago. Optimism, along with tenacity, ranked as her best traits, but she was filled with doubt.

Tempted to turn on her heels and scurry back to the van, she rapped again. An instant later, the door swung open. Kane still intimidated her with a look, she realized, feeling more nervous than she wanted to be. "Hi," she said with exaggerated brightness.

Deep-set eyes traveled down to her soaked and mud-spotted sneakers, then came back to her face. "What do you want?"

Rachel had used the moment to inch closer to the screen door, to breathe again. "It's been ages." She gave him her best smile. "I don't know if you remember me. I was friends with Marnie," she said, hoping the mention of his sister would stir his smile. "We—my family used to live here—in this house." When he said nothing, she went on, "Charlie Greer sold it to my parents. Before we moved to Texas, Charlie bought it back." As another chill gave her goose bumps, she contemplated what was the best way to get Heather into the warm house. "Do you remember me?"

He bore a five-o'clock shadow. It darkened his jaw, emphasized the shiny blackness of his hair, those pale-gray eyes. "I remember you." No friendliness entered those eyes, even when they slanted toward the pink bundle cradled in her arms. Had he trained himself to keep his face so expressionless, his emotions so unreadable? "If you're looking for my sister, I can't help you."

"This is kind of complicated. May we come in?" Rachel had been so anxious to see him that she'd never considered he might not be receptive to her. Had he always been so unfriendly? Years ago, blinded by infatuation, she'd never noticed anything except his muscles, those gray eyes and the sensation that quivered within her whenever he'd been near. "I really need to talk to you."

"About what?" Despite the question, he opened the screen door.

Edgy, Rachel gripped the straps of the diaper bag that she'd slung over her shoulder before leaving the van and scooted past him into the house. Behind her, she heard the click of the front door closing. Tension crept up again as she faced him. She couldn't blurt out words. Now because he acted so displeased with their intrusion, she felt stymied how to proceed. She could hardly thrust Heather at him with her news. *This baby is yours. Take her.*

With Heather's squeak, Rachel mentally returned to a more immediate concern. "I'm sorry, but I'll need to change and feed her, or in a minute she'll demonstrate her lung power."

He pointed to his left. "You can take her in there."

She knew what room he meant. It used to be her bedroom. An enormous room, she'd shared it with her younger sister, Gillian. She paused at the doorway. Her posters of rock stars, the collection of stuffed animals, the lovely, ruffled shams, the laced curtain and the patchwork quilt were gone. The room contained a bed with a bare mattress, a small chest of drawers and a rocking chair.

Bending over the bed, she unwrapped the pink blanket, then the pale-aqua lightweight one from Heather. "This was my room, mine and my sister's," she said, aware he'd followed and was standing in the doorway. It felt so strange to be in the room she'd called her own as a child. She'd never insisted on privacy from Gillian. She'd liked being in a room with her sister, especially on stormy days and nights. Rachel had hated to be alone. Her sister, daring and bolder even at a young age, had loved to sit with her nose pressed to the window and watch the sky explode with lightning.

"Are you almost done?" he asked, as if she'd said nothing.

It was best Heather was too young to understand any of this. Rachel removed the soiled diaper, then fastened a clean one. "Yes, I'm done," she replied while she maneuvered Heather's tiny feet into the fleece, peach-colored sleeper and zipped it. She dumped the soiled diaper into a plastic bag that she'd removed from the diaper bag and wiped her hands with a moist towelette.

Only once had he glanced at Heather. She remembered his father had been like this, curt and remote. An angry, morose man, he'd made Marnie cry with his harsh words. What if Kane had become his father? Would Marnie have wanted Heather to be with a man like that?

Kane eyed the baby in her arms, had already noted no wedding band. A baby and no husband. He'd never figured this kind of future for Rachel Quinn, then he'd never really known her. "There's coffee if you want a cup," he said, and walked out. He viewed her last few moments as a stall tactic. Whatever her problem was, she was struggling to spit it out. What bothered him most was why she was involving him.

"The coffee smells wonderful."

He looked back over his shoulder, made eye contact with her. He wondered where she'd left the baby. With a hand he motioned toward the coffee brewer. "There." He had no intention of waiting on her, making her feel welcomed. He caught a whiff of some light and lemony fragrance as she passed by to reach the coffeepot.

"That room is the one that I—"

"Grew up in," he finished for her. Turning, he braced his backside against the kitchen counter. "I know."

From across the table she stared quizzically at him. He couldn't blame her. He was being more curt than he intended. But annoyance had inched under his skin. Annoyance with himself for letting her into the house.

"When did Charlie die?" she asked between sips of coffee.

"It's been a while." Because he lived alone, he paid little attention to the house. With her there, scanning the room, he noticed the refrigerator needed wiping. Unlike Charlie, he had no housekeeper, wanted no one snooping around. "Why don't we cut to the chase. What do you want from me?"

"This is difficult."

"If this is about my sister, I haven't seen her in years." He wondered if Marnie had found all she'd wanted. Wherever she'd gone and whatever she'd done, she had to have found something better than they'd had here.

"I know."

"You know?" That caught his attention. "Does that mean you've seen her recently?"

Though Rachel remained unsure what to do about Heather, she had to tell him about his sister. Being the bearer of bad news was never easy. "Marnie was in Texas."

"In Texas?" He set down his cup and gave her his full attention. "How do you know that?"

"I was there." Rachel wanted to stop, plead a headache, illness—escape. How would she tell him? "I worked in a bank, and she came in for a job."

"She has a good job."

"She was a bank teller."

"She—" His face tensed.

She guessed her hesitation was irritating him, but how could she blurt out what needed to be said?

"Why do you keep saying…was?"

She could have told him that Marnie had chosen not to contact him. One night over dishes of rocky road ice cream, Marnie had cried and explained that she'd never wanted to burden her brother with her problems. "Kane, I'm sorry—"

"Sorry. What the hell are you sorry about?"

"Marnie died a week and a half ago." Rachel gave him a moment while the words registered. She prayed her voice didn't break, and she didn't cry. "I tried to contact you.'' She hurried an explanation. ''I knew from Lori—Lori Wolken—that you were still living here. I tried to reach you.'' She withdrew two papers she'd slipped earlier into her jeans pocket. ''When I couldn't, I called Lori with the news about Marnie. She told me that you weren't in town.''

Expressionless, he kept staring at her.

Rachel wished someone who knew him was here. ''I learned you returned from a two-week fishing trip yesterday.''

''How?'' A demand edged his voice. She could hear a silent message. *Explain this to me. Tell me this isn't real.* ''How did she die?''

Rachel set the folded death certificate for Marnie and a birth certificate for Heather on the table. ''Your sister was proud, really proud.'' Would he blame Rachel? She'd always felt as if she hadn't done enough, hadn't come up with good enough arguments to convince Marnie that she shouldn't have the baby at home, hadn't tried hard enough. If only she'd convinced Marnie to accept help, how different everything might be now.

''You didn't answer my question.''

The harsh command forced her head up. Such pain clouded his eyes. She wanted to touch him. ''I was her friend, but she wouldn't let me help. She always said she wouldn't take charity. I tried.'' Rachel felt the knot forming in her throat. ''I really did. But she wouldn't go to the hospital, wouldn't let me pay.''

''Hospital? She was ill?''

''Oh, no.'' Rachel wished she was standing closer, could touch him. ''Kane, she was pregnant. But instead of going to a hospital, she decided to have the baby at home.''

His shoulders raised, but that was the only visible change.

''She had a midwife come to the trailer.'' Rachel took a step closer. This was far more difficult than she'd imagined. ''There were complications. We called for an ambulance, and they rushed her to the hospital, but—''

He kept staring past her as if she were invisible.

''Before she reached the hospital, she was gone.''

''Why didn't she have it in the hospital? She had a job, medical insurance, didn't she?''

She had loved Marnie like a sister but wasn't blind to her faults and hoped he wasn't, either. ''She took off a lot and lost the job.'' She didn't wait for him to ask why. ''There was a man. She wanted to be with him.''

His jaw tightened slightly, but he held on to a stone face.

Rachel presumed he'd mastered that look when he was young. ''Kane, I'm so sorry. If there's anything I can do—''

His deep-set eyes came back to her. ''Was she scared?''

The memory of that night closed in on Rachel again. ''I don't think so.'' She felt tears smarting at the back of her eyes and grabbed a deep breath. Tears now would do no good. ''She wasn't really aware,'' Rachel added. ''It all happened so fast.'' Her voice trailed off. She was talking to his back. ''Wait,'' she said before he reached the door. She wasn't insensitive to his need to be alone. She wished she could have offered some kind of solace, but what could she have said? That evening had been awful, frightening. She'd lost a wonderful friend. But it didn't matter what either of them felt. Heather had to come first for both of them. ''What about Marnie's baby?''

Chapter Two

Silence hung in the air. Seconds on the kitchen wall clock ticked by with excruciating slowness before he swung back, before those eyes locked on hers. "Baby?"

No, he didn't look baffled. He looked dazed. As much as she wished she could give him time to mourn, she had to make him understand. Heather existed. If he didn't accept his obligation— She let the thought die for a moment, hating to think of Heather as an obligation. But his acceptance of his responsibility for Heather might be the little one's only hope for a life that didn't include foster homes. "Heather— the baby is Marnie's. You're her uncle."

As if someone had poked him hard in the back, it straightened. "So you say."

What did that mean? Didn't he believe her? "I'm telling the truth."

In anger most people shouted, he spoke low. "You come here with a story about my sister and a baby. Okay, I don't doubt my sister is—" He paused, his gaze dropping to the folded sheets of paper on the table. In an abrupt move he picked them up and unfolded one. Absently he ran a thumb over the seal of Texas on the paper confirming his sister's death. "Okay. My sister is…gone. You'd have no reason to lie about that."

She heard a silent but. "You don't think I'm telling the truth about Heather?"

"The baby could be yours. You could be trying to pawn it off as Marnie's."

"Pawn it off!" Fury rose so swiftly Rachel thought she'd lose her good sense and take a swing at him. "She's your sister's baby. Not mine." He had no idea how much it hurt her to say that, how often she'd made herself remember that, since she had started caring for Heather. If he saw Heather's gray eyes, eyes so like his own, or touched her and felt the velvety soft skin, he would never turn away from her. But he hadn't even seen her yet. "Heather is yours."

Before she could utter a protest, she watched him snag a rain slicker from a hook by the door. A second later it closed behind him. How could he walk away? Heather was his flesh and blood. He was the only one she had. How could he be so unfeeling, so indifferent? And what should she do now? She had no choices, she realized.

Planning to return to the motel for the night, she

went to the bedroom and lifted Heather into her arms. Because of Kane's reaction, misgivings about him nagged at her. Rachel drew Heather closer, wishing for some way to know she was making the right decisions for her.

Since that night, she'd become responsible for Heather. She'd been the one who'd first held Marnie's baby. She'd cuddled the newborn close while the midwife had frantically tried to save Marnie's life. After a call to 911, with paramedics crowding Marnie, Rachel had wandered to a far end of the room, rocking the newborn and praying for her friend.

No one's fault. An unexpected rise in Marnie's blood pressure. A cerebral hemorrhage. It would have happened at any time. Those were the words said to Rachel. Her friend's life had been a thin thread, ready to snap. That knowledge had been small consolation.

Rachel had lost a best friend, a woman she'd been as close to as her sister, Gillian. And as Rachel would do for her brother or sister, she would have done anything for Marnie. With her gone, that loyalty transferred to Marnie's baby, to a child she was struggling not to get too attached to.

Rain slowed to a drizzle by the time Kane reached Tulley's Bar. His skin and hair damp, he straddled a stool at the scarred wooden bar and downed a whisky quickly, letting the heat burn his throat while he read the death certificate once more.

Because his old man had been a drunkard, Kane drank cautiously and never set foot in Tulley's before sunset. Too many times his father had reached for a drink to start his day.

He stared at the amber liquid in his glass while he fought a myriad of feelings. The shock from Rachel's words settled over him. It seemed unreal, impossible. Marnie was gone. His stomach muscles clenched. It didn't matter that she hadn't been in his life for more than a decade. He'd believed she was somewhere else, that her life was better than the living hell they'd shared with their old man after their mother had died. But Marnie wasn't happier. She was gone. He would never see her again.

He wanted to vent anger, but who deserved it? And to give in to a softer emotion never occurred to him. He'd blocked any urge to cry when his mother had died. Losing someone else close to him only reinforced something he'd always known. There was danger in letting the heart feel too much.

So what now? Did Rachel have his sister's belongings? Who'd paid for the funeral? And what about the kid? Was it really his sister's? If it was, what would he do with it?

At seven the next morning Kane had no answers. Even before he opened his eyes, he cursed the sound of rain thudding against the roof in a steady, syncopated beat. Through his bedroom window he saw the dreary gray sky. In no hurry he stretched on the bed, then roused himself. Rain had canceled yesterday's tours. Today the *Sea Siren* would be stuck at dock all day. Yawning, he yanked on jeans and tugged a T-shirt over his head.

In the kitchen he plugged in the coffee brewer. On the table were the papers Rachel had given him. He unfolded the birth certificate. Heather Riley. He noted that someone had typed the word *unknown* on the line for the father's name. The seal of Texas made the document legal. He closed his fingers around it. Calmer now, he could talk sensibly to Rachel. With only half a dozen motels in town, he assumed he'd have no problem finding her.

He gave himself half an hour to nurse a couple of cups of coffee, shower and shave, then drove his truck down Main Street toward the *Sea Siren* to talk to his deckhand before he started his search.

Instead of going to the boat first, as he spotted Rachel's van parked outside Benny's Café, he negotiated the truck into an adjacent parking lot. No amount of avoidance would work. He parked his truck and strolled toward the café. Through its windows, he saw her.

Head bowed, she sat in one of the blue vinyl booths. As he opened the café door, the bell above it jingled. The café was decorated in blue and white. A breakfast crowd, mostly locals, occupied the stools at the counter and several tables. Heads swiveled toward Kane before he shut the door behind him. He received no nods of hello, no smiles. He never expected any.

People believed he was his father's child, and Ian Riley had ranked low on everyone's list of favorite people by the time he'd died. For good reasons, they'd claimed. He'd come to town, sweet-talked Kathleen Feenley, and got her pregnant. He'd ruined a good girl. But no one had really objected to him until he'd become an embarrassment, the town drunk.

Then Kane had committed his own offense. He didn't need their condemnations. He damned himself whenever he thought about Charlie's last day.

Ignoring stares, he weaved a path around some tables to reach Rachel. Though no sun shone through the windows, she looked sunny. He figured it was a visual thing. She wore faded jeans and a bright yellow top that clung gently to the curves of her breasts. Because too many emotions remained close to the surface, he steeled himself when he saw sympathy in her expression. "Guess we need to talk."

"Sometimes it's difficult for me to believe Marnie's gone," she said with a world of hurt in her voice that made Kane certain she wasn't giving lip service but was telling the truth. "This must be such a hard time for you."

"A shock," he said candidly. He figured that this woman, with her overabundance of kindness and too-caring manner, set herself up to be hurt easily. While he slid into the booth across from her, she angled to her left. Was the baby there? Was it a boy or girl? A girl. He recalled Rachel saying "she" when in need of a place to change the diaper.

"I—" She closed her mouth when Rosie Furnam, the oldest of the café's waitresses, a grandmother with a love for gossip, came near.

"Do you want something?" She looked less than pleased.

Kane never ate in town, hadn't for years since

Charlie had died. For meals out, he would drive to one of the towns nearby. "Nothing."

"More coffee?" she asked Rachel.

Briefly Rachel's eyes met his before raising to Rosie's questioning stare. "No, thank you."

Kane waited until Rosie finally sauntered away. "Tell me what happened to my sister."

Rachel explained what the doctors in the emergency room had told her.

No one's fault. Those words gave Kane no comfort. He glanced at the wall of windows, away from the soft compassion in the green eyes studying him. He wanted none of it. "You handled the funeral, you said."

As if it pained her, she avoided meeting his eyes. "We had a small memorial service." She concentrated on the dark liquid in her cup. "Several people from the trailer court, and former co-workers came."

He didn't want to know the details. "Let me know how much I owe you." When she raised her head, he sensed she planned a protest. "She was my sister." *My responsibility.* Except he'd forgotten that, hadn't he? "And if I owe you anything else—"

"Please. She was my friend." Moisture glistened in her eyes. "A wonderful friend. I'd have done anything for her. I wanted her to go to the hospital." She was rambling as if trying to understand what went wrong. "I had money saved. She could have gone."

Despite years of separation, Kane knew his sister wouldn't take a handout from anyone. He wasn't sure she'd have even welcomed help from him. They'd had to accept too much charity as kids. "She always was stubborn. If she didn't want to take your help, you couldn't have done anything to change her mind.''

"Thank you. I know you're trying to make me feel better, but—''

"I'm not doing anything,'' he countered, because he wasn't trying to offer comfort. Instinctively her chin rose a notch. Better she was offended. He didn't need this woman as a friend. If she'd thought he planned to make this easy, she was wrong.

"I was telling the truth. Heather is Marnie's,'' she said softer as if suddenly aware how many people were staring at them.

"Marnie named her?'' Less stunned, he admitted now that he really hadn't doubted her. She'd have had no reason to lie about the baby, and like the death certificate for his sister, a birth certificate for the baby forced the truth on him.

"Heather was the name she'd said she liked best, the one I used for her baptism. Do you like it?''

He shrugged a shoulder. "It's fine. Who's the father? He wasn't named on the birth certificate.''

Rachel toyed with a spoon. "I really don't know.''

"Why don't you?'' Settling back in the booth, he stretched denim-clad legs beneath the table. "You claim you and my sister were good friends.''

Inches from them, Rosie lingered at a table. Revealing discretion, Rachel waited for the waitress to move away. "We were. But Marnie never told me the father's name. I asked, but she wouldn't tell me.''

"How did you get the baby?''

"During her pregnancy, Marnie had written a note,

had it notarized. It gave me temporary guardianship until Heather was with you. That protected her, kept her from falling into the system.'' A slim, almost shy smile curved her lips. ''I rushed here with her before anyone challenged the paper.''

He'd guess she was one of those honest-to-the-core people who didn't even park illegally.

Her gaze shifted to the window. ''The rain's stopped.'' Vacationers' cars lined the town's main street, bumper to bumper. Summer tourists ambled along the sidewalks now, drawn to the souvenir shops and art galleries.

Inside the café, they'd become the center of attention. Regulars at the counter stared their way. One of the waitresses cleared a table at a snail's pace instead of getting an order to the cook's counter. Kane thought the woman across from him needed to know. ''Being with me isn't the popular thing to do.''

Rachel met his stare with an equally steady one. ''It never was. I was warned years ago to keep my distance from you.'' She sounded slightly amused. ''You were 'the wild one,''' she said, a laugh definitely lacing her voice.

Eyes darted their way again. Questioning looks fixed on them when Rachel sounded as if she was having fun with Kane. As Rachel slid out of the booth, he expected one of the town's do-gooders to rush over and deliver a warning about him. Bending forward, she grabbed the handle of the cushioned seat that held the baby and lifted it. Kane couldn't see his sister's child.

''I'm not fifteen now. I prefer to make my own

judgments. I'll see you at the house," she said, loudly enough for everyone to hear.

He considered grabbing her arm, telling her there was no more to be said. But with her comment he imagined the shock rippling through the people seated at the tables and counter. If he caused a confrontation, he'd just make her grist for the gossip mill. He didn't care what anyone thought, but he had enough guilt to bear without being responsible for the town ostracizing her for getting involved with him. No, thanks. He didn't need any of this. His life had been simple, and he planned to keep it that way.

At the house Rachel stood on the porch, waiting for Kane. Her hand remained clenched around the handle of the baby carrier. At her feet was a suitcase and a bag, bigger than the denim one draped over her shoulder. This one was decorated with pink and blue ducks.

When he climbed out of his truck, she moved closer to the porch railing. "I have all of her things in the van."

How much could someone that small have? Stalling, he stopped by the mailbox at the curb. They needed to talk this out now. She needed to understand that he had no room in his life for the baby. "She's not staying," he said as much for Rachel's benefit as a confirmation that this was best.

As he joined her on the porch, he saw disbelief sweep across her face. "You won't take her?"

He'd thought his problem was obvious. How could he take her? "I don't know anything about babies."

"That's not really a problem. You can learn."

He figured she was afflicted with the rose-colored-glasses syndrome. It didn't matter that this child was his sister's, that some part of her could be back in his life. "She belongs with her father, not me."

A brisk wind cut a path through the porch. It whipped at her hair and flapped at the lightweight jacket she wore as if sensing a frail opponent. "I told you." She hunched her shoulders. "I don't know who that is."

Kane shoved the house key into the lock and opened the door for her. "Then we'll need to find him. Any ideas about where to start?"

She raised a hand, swiped at strands flying across her cheek. "I'd be guessing. I think he's one of three men she dated on and off during the past two years."

An urge to touch the silky-looking strands crept over him. "Why didn't she tell you who the father was?" Shifting his stance, he blocked the wind from her and the baby. "I thought friends told friends everything."

"Do you?"

He could have told her he had none. He didn't allow himself that kind of closeness with anyone anymore. "It's going to take time to find the baby's father." Because he wasn't any more father material than his own dad, he asked a logical question. "What do you expect me to do with her?"

Worry rushed Rachel. She crossed her fingers and toes. She didn't know what she would do if he refused. "Well—arrangements need to be made—to care for her. You could hire a nanny."

"Why not you?" he asked, snatching up the pink-and-blue duck bag and the suitcase.

"Oh, no, not me." Already she'd spent too much time with Heather. It was one thing to bring Heather to him, quite another to stay, care for her daily. She preceded him into the house. "I need to return to Texas."

"Married?"

Rachel shot a look back at him. "No, I'm not but—"

"I can't stay home with her," he said, not giving her time to offer reasons. "Someone needs to be here."

Rachel wondered what he thought she did to pay rent. "I never intended to stay. I have my job. I—"

He moved and dropped several envelopes and a magazine on a circular maple end table. "Then you'd better have another idea. Because you can't come here, drop all of this in my lap and take off."

Rachel scowled at him in vain. Head bent, he was sorting through the envelopes. What he'd said was exactly what she'd planned to do. One evening Marnie had insisted on talking about what-ifs. If something happened to her, she wanted Rachel to be her baby's temporary guardian until she took the baby to its uncle. "Keep the baby until she's with Kane, until you're sure she's where she'll be happy," she'd said.

A week later Marnie was dead, and Rachel's lightly made promise had become a vow of forever. But what if the two promises didn't go hand in hand? "I'm sorry, but I'm not the answer to your problem." Her voice trailed off as those gray eyes fixed on her. She didn't know what was more disconcerting—being ignored or having those eyes on her.

"What do you do?"

"I'm in charge of customer investments." His brows knit with a questioning look. "Mutual funds, IRAs, annuities," Rachel explained.

"So how did you get time off?"

She'd had to. She'd promised her best friend she'd take care of her baby. "After Heather was born, I took a leave of absence because I wasn't sure when I'd be back. And I stayed home to be with her and to make arrangements, find you. Legally she's yours, not mine now, because I did find you."

"I can't care for her by myself." He waited a second as if giving his words time to sink in. "I can hire someone until I find the father, but that won't happen by tomorrow."

"There are a lot of wonderful people in this town," Rachel reminded him. "They'll help—"

"They won't help me."

Rachel puzzled over that. "Why wouldn't they?"

For a long moment he held her gaze with an unflinching one. "If you leave, so does the baby," he said instead of answering her.

He couldn't mean that. "How can you—" She heard her own anxiousness and paused, drew a deep breath.

"You want what's best for her, don't you?"

What was his point? "Of course, I do."

"I'm not it."

Her shoulders slumped. She didn't know if that was true. But Marnie hadn't believed that. Seeing the stubborn set of his jaw, she knew he meant what he'd said. She was torn. She needed to protect herself. She could only do that by leaving. He had no idea what he was asking of her. She cast a look at Heather asleep in the infant carrier seat. She was so innocent. Someone had to protect her, too.

If she kept her guard up, she could help them, couldn't she? *Stop! Stop thinking about yourself. Think about the baby. The baby needs you.* She remembered how hard it had been for her sister and brother when they'd lost their parents. Though she'd had some difficult times supporting and raising them, she'd done her best to hold them together. She'd known that the more love a child had, the better off the child would be. So she gave them all she could. Heather, too, needed that until Kane found Heather's biological father or became the daddy Heather needed. "I'll stay until you hire a nanny."

"Fine."

There was such a ring of satisfaction in his voice. "You expected me to change my mind, didn't you?" Rachel challenged.

"You lead with your heart." He looked down, checked his watch, offered no more explanation. "I have to leave."

She assumed with the sky more blue and filled now with lighter, fluffier clouds that he had a tour or a fishing trip.

"Here's a key to the house." He detached a key from a ring. "We'll need to get another made."

Before she changed her mind, Rachel accepted it,

but she hadn't considered that a yes meant living with him.

"If you need help hauling anything in, leave it, and I'll do it when I get back."

She didn't bother to ask where he was going or how long he'd be gone. With the closing of the door, she stretched for a breath, glad to be alone. He'd disturbed her more than a decade ago. And still did.

Get over it, she told herself while scanning the room. She was here to stay for a few days. But never had she expected to live in this house again. Clasping the key, she eyed the blue Early-American-style sofa. The furniture he'd chosen was an eclectic mix of Early American, Cape Cod and thrift store specials, though the blue sofa and a chair worked together, and the seascape over the fireplace was a blend of blues that suited the room.

Looking around, she could almost see her mother standing by the front window with its endless view of the ocean. Sounds of her brother and sister affectionately squabbling hung in the air. Near the fireplace an image came alive of her father petting the family dog, a black lab.

She loved the house, probably because some of the most wonderful days of her life had passed here with her parents and sister and brother. They'd been a family in the true sense, sharing love and laughter.

Family. She'd always wanted that. Other girls talked about careers, not Rachel. She'd always wanted a family of her own—husband, children. By now she'd thought that she'd be married, have that family, but so much of what she'd yearned for had passed her by. She couldn't have regrets. There was no going back, no chance to recapture those dreams, and dwelling over what would never happen was a waste of time.

Curious to see if the house had changed, she lifted Heather's infant seat and went into the kitchen. She'd explore the other rooms later. Stark, the room contained a round, dark-wood table and chairs, and a nineteenth-century corner cupboard. She stared at the shelf above French doors. Her mother had displayed her collection of nineteenth-century Staffordshire children's plates and mugs on it. Now it was bare. There were no frills, no knickknacks, no decorative touches. The house of a no-nonsense man, Rachel gathered.

She placed Heather's carrier on the floor by the kitchen table, then began opening and closing cabinet doors to locate coffee. Sparse, the cabinets contained only a few dishes and staples, enough food for one person to keep from starving. The refrigerator held eggs, beer, a few cans of soda, a bottle of good wine and cheese.

After finding the coffee, she started the coffee brewer, then reached for the telephone on a wall near the back door. Before she'd left Texas, she'd phoned her brother and sister. They'd both insisted she call collect when she located Kane.

Rachel stalled, waiting until the coffee finished hissing, then poured herself a cup while she prepared for her brother's arguments. Sean had been concerned about her making the trip, about taking on the responsibility of Heather, but Rachel had assured her brother that everything was temporary. He would *not* be happy to hear she was staying.

His brother's brief businesslike greeting preceded a beep. She left a cheery message, including her new phone number on his answering machine, then punched out Gillian's phone number. The phone rang ten times. Who knew where her footloose sister was? Still Rachel tried again five minutes later while drinking a second cup of coffee.

"Hello," a bright, happy voice greeted. People claimed Gillian resembled a redheaded Meg Ryan. Rachel didn't see the physical resemblance. But both women were slim built, bubbly and had a sparkle in their eyes.

"Hello, yourself," Rachel said.

"Hey, big sister. How are you? I was thinking about calling you. I have a new job, a modeling job in San Francisco."

"Modeling?"

"For a hairstylist at a convention, so I'll be leaving Los Angeles this weekend. I'll let you know if I end up with orange or magenta hair." She breezed on without taking a breath. "I assume you found Kane."

"Yes. I'll be staying in Hubbard Bay a little longer. What about Hawaii?" Since getting her small-plane pilot's license nearly two years ago, Gillian had been looking for the "perfect job." It had come last week. A charter plane company needed another pilot.

"I don't go for another three months," she answered. "So why are you staying?"

Rachel explained the situation with Kane.

"You're living with him?"

"He's gone most of the day," Rachel was quick to remind her. *Don't ask what I'm doing.* It sounded insane, she knew. She was living with a man she didn't know, for an indefinite amount of time, to protect a baby she didn't want to get too close to. The situation was ludicrous.

"Sean was worried you'd get attached. Did you call him?"

"I left a message."

"He won't be pleased."

No, he wouldn't be, Rachel knew. Even though he was three years younger than her, he'd become as protective as a big brother since he'd become an adult. "I'm not attached. I could hardly leave Heather with a man who knows absolutely nothing about babies."

"So you'll stay there until he does?"

Rachel shared with her Kane's plan to find Heather's father. "I'll be here until he hires a nanny or finds the right man. I'm not certain that he'd be best for Heather."

"You think she should stay with Kane?"

Now there was a question. "I don't know."

"Such indecisiveness is so unlike you, Rachel. You usually know what you're doing at every moment."

"This is a different situation."

A smile sprang into her voice. "I'm glad you're not being too logical."

"I'm being logical," Rachel countered but didn't feel defensive, aware her sister, who was a relentless tease, was having fun at her expense. "The baby needs someone with experience to care for her."

"You know, it's all right if you don't act sensible all the time. For too many years, you had to think about the consequences of everything for you, Sean and me. You need to enjoy. Wing it."

Rachel laughed. "*Wing* it?"

"Do something adventurous."

"And you should show some caution," Rachel returned.

Another bubbly laugh came through the phone. "Got to go now, sis."

Rachel shook her head, aware Gillian lacked even a smidgen of caution. Lovable and unpredictable, she lived for the moment. Rachel rattled off Kane's phone number to her sister and elicited Gillian's promise to call when she reached San Francisco. Do something adventurous, she'd said. Wasn't staying with a stranger adventurous enough for a woman who lived an orderly, well-thought-out life?

Chapter Three

At thirty-one, Rachel would admit that she had
fallen into a rut before all this had happened. While
her brother worked for a prestigious Boston law firm,
and Gillian was still finding herself but was happy
with a lifestyle that included traveling, Rachel had
settled for what she had, a home in Texas, a job at
the bank. She wasn't unhappy. She had friends, a satisfying job, but there would always be an emptiness
in her life. Always.

While Heather finished her nap, Rachel opened the
front door to cart in the portable crib and clothes, but
the rain had started again. She saw no point in getting
soaked. Deciding to wait until the rain eased, she gave
in to her curiosity about the house, wanting to see all
the rooms, see if they looked the same, sparked memories.

At the end of the short hall was a sparsely decorated, masculine room. On the bed was a homemade dark-blue-and-white patchwork quilt. Had his mother or some other relative made it? On top of a small, round, mahogany table near the window was a photograph. Even from a distance Rachel recognized Marnie's school photo. In a corner of the room was a three-shelf mahogany bookcase filled mostly with paperbacks. She'd have liked to step in, but felt she'd be invading his privacy.

Instead she crossed into the room that used to be her brother's. On a clear day its window offered a view of a distant lighthouse, of the endless water. Rachel circled the empty room. In the closet was a pull-down ladder for the attic. Of all the rooms, this one was the most perfect for a nursery. She could imagine Kane's expression if she hauled all of Heather's belongings into it. No, for now she would keep Heather in the room near her.

She returned to the kitchen and groped in her shoulder bag for a paperback to read while she waited for the rain to end. The plan had made sense then, but by late afternoon a downpour had begun.

With little choice Rachel placed Heather in the middle of the bed, comforted that a newborn stayed still, and after fishing her van keys from her shoulder bag, she slipped on her rain slicker and headed for the door. Though she loved walking in the rain, she didn't like storms. She was still wishing that she could avoid going out when she opened the door.

"Where are you going?"

She jumped, then laughed at herself as Kane stood

before her. ''Out there.'' She gestured with her hand at the air and in the direction behind him. ''You scared me silly,'' she said on a laugh.

''Sorry.''

''It's okay.'' He stood so near that she smelled the rain on him. She never lied to herself and wouldn't start now. The quickening of her pulse had as much to do with a sensual reaction as it had to do with skittishness because he'd appeared so suddenly before her. ''I need to get Heather's portable crib,'' she said loudly to be heard over the hammering rain.

''Give me your keys.'' The wind ruffled his hair, flapped at the hem of his yellow slicker. ''I'll get it.''

''That's very nice of—'' She didn't bother to finish as he curled his fingers around the keys dangling from her hand and thrust a pizza carton at her. For only a moment she peered through the sheet of slanting rain and watched him sprint to the van.

This stay was not going to be easy, she decided as she shut the door. He was fascinating and annoying. One moment he came across as thoughtful and considerate, the next he bordered on brusque, almost unpleasant. He'd always been mysterious to her. He'd been a brooding, quiet boy who'd smiled rarely and usually only at his sister. But he'd warmed Rachel all the way down to her toes with that smile.

Grinning over her own thought, she set the pizza on the counter. Unable to resist, she peeked at it with a deep inhalation. It smelled heavenly. She swiped a piece of sausage from one slice, reclosed the box, then made her way to the bedroom to check on Heather.

Fortunately she snoozed, undisturbed by the

weather and her surroundings. Shadows danced on the walls. The wind whistled through the old house, wiggled doors, banged shutters. Rachel decided that only an ungrateful fool wouldn't appreciate what Kane was doing.

While waiting for him, she moved the infant seat and oversize diaper bag to make a spot for the crib. A soft bang, a muttered oath made her look up. Rain plastered his hair. Glossy, dark strands flared out in unruly curls below his ears. Raindrops beaded his face. "I appreciate your help." She noticed that he'd shrugged out of his rain gear somewhere on his way to her.

"You don't have to keep thanking me." He snapped open a side of the collapsed crib, then unclipped the other side of the bed. "Hell, you're the one who's been put out." He pressed on the rail of the crib as if testing its steadiness. "I'll get you sheets for your bed."

He was acting more pleasant. Rachel hoped this was a new phase, one that would last for a while. While he was gone, she dug a crib sheet for the crib out of a suitcase and made up a bed for Heather. Though sleeping, her mouth puckered, made sucking noises as Rachel shifted her from the big bed to the smaller one. "You're getting hungry, aren't you?" she cooed. Peripherally she caught movement and looked up to see Kane set snow-white sheets on the top of a badly scratched walnut dresser.

"Does she ever answer?"

Had that actually been humor? "No, but eventually she will."

His eyes strayed to the crib. He looked baffled. "She's sleeping again?"

Rachel veiled a smile. Until that moment she hadn't thought he'd looked at Heather. That he was showing some interest in his niece meant progress. "Infants do a lot of that. That and eating." She thought better about mentioning the dozens of diaper changes.

"If you say so."

The sudden coolness surprised her. Had he drummed it up because he thought he was showing too much interest in Heather? Who knew what he was thinking. He wasn't an easy man to understand. She usually preferred men who willingly carried on conversations, showed some sensitivity, weren't so difficult to read. He really wasn't her type, she acknowledged. Of course he wasn't, but that didn't stop her from staring at how his jeans snugly hugged his tight backside.

"If you're hungry, there's pizza."

Fortunately she managed to stop staring before he turned around. "I'm starving. I didn't have much breakfast before coming here." Her stomach churning in anticipation now, she followed him to the kitchen. While he opened the refrigerator, she moved the carton to the center of the table. "I'm glad you thought of this."

"I knew there wasn't anything in the house."

She'd nearly said the same thing but thought he might believe she was insulting him.

With the refrigerator door open, he held out a can of soda. "This or beer or—"

"This is fine." Rachel took the can of soda. "I thought everything would look different here, but not much has changed," she said to encourage him to talk.

He swung toward her, shutting the refrigerator door with his forearm. "People like it that way."

Rachel looked down and yanked the tab on the can of soda. "I know." When he straddled a chair, she joined him at the table. "It was always such a wonderful town. I'm glad it hasn't changed." Rachel glanced toward the window as lightning flashed again and brightened the darkness outside. She drew in one of those long breaths that was meant to calm a person.

Across the table from her, he gave her a long, searching look. "The storm bothers you."

She hated to make the admittance. She was a grown-up, not six years old. "Sometimes. You must be busy as captain of two boats," she said, searching for something that would keep conversation flowing. "Do you have a crew?"

"A small one. Lonnie Culhern's my first mate."

"I know who that is," Rachel said as she recalled Lonnie, a blond Adonis type. Good-looking and muscular, he attracted women with little effort. "The girls liked him."

Balancing a slice of pizza on his fingertips, he took a bite before answering. "Skirt chasing only ranks second behind fishing in his life."

Rachel smiled. Despite the quip, his voice had carried a note of fondness. "You like him a lot."

"He's been around a long while," he said, instead of commenting about what she'd said.

Did that mean he was close with him or not? Puzzled, Rachel concentrated on the pizza. Was there no bond between them, or was he one of those people who never allowed himself to admit that he cared about someone? Worry for Heather skittered through her. How would she fare with a man who so tightly guarded his emotions?

The scrape of chair legs on the linoleum made her look up. From a kitchen drawer he removed a candle and matches.

"Do you expect the power to go off?"

He didn't need to answer. Lights flickered once more. The room went black. She heard the strike of a match then. When he turned with a candle in his hand, it cast an eerie glow over his face.

"Sit still," he said, setting the candle in the middle of the table.

"I'm not going anywhere." Unaccustomed to where furniture was in the house, she thought it would be dumb to move around and bump into things.

The beam of a flashlight suddenly swept the room. "Here." He offered one to her.

As Rachel reached for it, his fingers lightly brushed hers. The contact was nothing, but unexpected warmth shot through her. She pulled back her hand. "Thank you." The reaction seemed silly, but, a little space from him, a little time to think clearly wouldn't do any harm. "I'd better check on Heather before I go to bed."

Aiming the flashlight, she ventured down the dark

hallway to the bathroom. It had been so long since she'd thought about any man in any way except as a friend. Perhaps that's why she'd felt something. She'd probably overreacted.

In the darkness she bent over Heather and gathered her in her arms. Listening to the raging storm, she perched on the edge of the bed, and soothingly skimmed a hand over Heather's soft, dark hair until her eyes closed. Possibly what she'd felt with Kane had been about old feelings.

Though she was tempted to keep holding Heather, she lowered her to her crib. Every time she cuddled the baby, her defenses weakened. Wasn't this what worried her brother most? He knew her soft heart. He knew how easily she could let Heather into her heart if she wasn't careful. But she was careful now. During one year of her life she'd endured a lifetime of pain and losses. She'd vowed then—never again.

For a moment Rachel peered out the window at the branches swaying beneath a violent wind. Before she spooked herself, she made up the bed, then changed into a pale-peach, silky nightshirt and climbed beneath the sheet. She didn't need to keep herself awake all night with imaginary fear. She had plenty of real problems to face tomorrow, like how to make a home here for Heather.

Crazy. His whole world had tipped and gone crazy, Kane decided the next morning as he stood on the deck of the *Maggie Lee*. In one day his solitary existence had been swept away. He tried to assure himself that it was temporary. But already his sleep had been interrupted by the baby's lusty wail in the middle of the night. Briefly he'd worried something was wrong with her, then as she quickly quieted, he'd assumed Rachel had control of the moment. He was glad someone did, because it sure as hell wasn't him.

They'd taken over his life in less than twenty-four hours. Cans of baby formula lined a shelf in his refrigerator, the sweet smell of some kind of baby powder hung in the air of the bedroom they occupied.

Then there was Rachel. She pulled at him with those soft-green eyes, with that smile, with that gentle, smooth voice.

"See you, Captain," a voice called out.

Kane yanked himself back to his surroundings. He nodded in response to the man passing by. A corporate-type in his white baseball cap, polo shirt and Bermuda shorts, he shared a fishing story with his friend while they sauntered toward their luxury cars. They'd spent early-morning hours on the water for the thrill of catching a big one.

Lonnie Culhern, his first mate, stood on the pier. He'd dropped out of college years ago to the dismay of his family who'd perceived their son as a Harvard graduate. After moving around like a rolling stone, he'd settled again in Hubbard Bay and had taken a job with Kane. Though comfortable with Lonnie's company, Kane had doubted his deckhand's staying power and kept a check on any real friendship developing between them.

"Heard a woman, new in town, was asking about you." A mixture of curiosity and speculation had entered Lonnie's voice. "According to Ephraim," he said about the owner of the town's oldest gas station, "she's a Quinn. Rachel Quinn. And a looker." An interested look spread over Lonnie's face. "Who is she? An old girlfriend?"

Kane squinted against a bright morning sun. "Never dated her."

"Ephraim said she's really something. Before I could ask more, Phil showed up and said we needed rain," he said with the annoyance he'd felt then. "That set off Ephraim who said sunshine was good for tourists, and Phil crabbed about us needing less instead of more of them. You know how they go on."

Kane nodded distractedly, figured they'd spent enough time talking about Rachel. She wasn't one of them anymore.

"Someone said she took care of her brother and sister after her parents died."

Kane continued to hose down the deck. "You turning into one of the town's gossips?"

Lonnie scowled as if he'd been insulted. "Just telling you what I heard."

"She has a kid." Purposely he led Lonnie astray.

As expected that news backed Lonnie up. Any hint of commitment scared the daylights out of him. "Whoa. Bad news." Completing his chore, he dropped a bag of trash, mostly beer cans into a nearby receptacle. "No wonder you're keeping your distance," he said before sauntering away from Kane.

Keeping his distance? Hardly.

Rachel had spent the morning playing catch up on sleep. She'd felt more rested than she'd expected, and except for Heather's usual 2 a.m. feeding, she'd slept through the night, able to ignore the storm.

She bathed Heather, emptied her suitcase and hung the clothes in the closet, but whiled away the rest of the day. By three o'clock she hadn't accomplished anything else. The mistake she made was digging into her shoulder bag for a piece of peppermint candy. Once her fingers curled over the paperback in her purse, she hadn't budged from the chair until after the author had her protagonist discover the first murder.

A touch annoyed with herself, Rachel grabbed her keys and made her way to the front door, intending on bringing Heather's things in from the van, then going to the store for formula. She took only one step onto the porch.

At some time earlier Kane had taken her keys from the kitchen counter where she'd dropped them. Before leaving for the boat, he must have brought to the porch the bouncing exerciser that resembled a car, an infant swing, and several boxes filled with baby clothing and blankets.

Rachel left all of it there, certain no one would take anything. The late-afternoon air carried a pleasant warmth. Hours ago the sun had burned away the mist off the Atlantic Ocean.

She pushed Heather's navy-colored stroller with its blue-and-white-striped canopy across the street and strolled along the cliff walk that traveled parallel with the water. She took in the rocky cliffs, the water crowded with boats sparkling beneath the sunlight. Everything from the smell of the salt-scented breeze to the sight of the deserted, weathered wood shacks made her feel at home. A gentle breeze whipped through her hair. Several gulls trailed a boat, skimmed the water for food.

Little had changed in the sixteen years since she'd left Hubbard Bay. It had maintained its small-town appearance. Generations of families lived in the town. Store owners passed businesses on to their children. Progress and expensive condos for summer tourists sprang up at more picturesque towns.

Hubbard Bay beckoned the tourist who wanted to see authentic New England, yearned for the feel of the ocean on the skin, viewed the weathered clapboard houses as quaint, instead of shabby. She'd spent years in Texas, longing for the smell of the ocean and wondered now how she would ever leave it again.

For the next hour she browsed along the part of Main Street's string of cottages that were used for businesses, mostly antique shops, though intermingled between them stood an insurance company, a baby store, a clothing boutique and several souvenir shops.

Feeling more content, more at peace than she had in ages, she strolled into the grocery store for formula. Though groceries were needed, she wanted to talk to Kane first about his food preferences. That Velma wasn't working made her feel as if she'd gotten a reprieve from the woman's interrogation.

In a good mood, she took a different route back to the house. She'd breathed a sigh of relief too soon, she realized. She was almost at the walkway of the house when she spotted Velma. Politeness forced Rachel to stop, but she eyed the house, wondering how to make a quick escape.

"Nice to see you again, Rachel. Did you get settled in?"

"Yes, I—"

"Guess you found Kane Riley since you're staying there," she said with a backhand wave at the house.

"Guess so," Rachel responded, not surprised that where she was staying was public knowledge.

Bending slightly forward, Velma scrutinized Heather's carriage with the removable infant seat. "Newfangled-type thing." The lines in the woman's face deepened. "Will your husband be coming?"

Rachel knew her answer, an honest one, would travel over the gossip grapevine faster than the speed of light. "I'm not married." She should have clarified everything, told Velma that the baby was Marnie's, but she wasn't in a mood for explanations.

"I see," was all the woman said.

Rachel took a step toward the house. She could make a mad dash for it, but that seemed silly. "I need to go in now, Velma. It's almost time for Heather's bottle."

"He got that house, got everything of Charlie Greer's after the old man died, you know," Velma said before she'd taken another step. "Of course, that was Kane Riley's fault." Rachel didn't miss the slight shift in the woman's mouth as if she'd just sniffed something disdainful. "What's that thing on the porch? One of those things the baby bounces in?"

Frowning at her words, Rachel traced the woman's stare to the bright-yellow car on the porch. "Yes."

Velma's scowl deepened. "Little young for that, isn't she?"

"It was given as a shower gift for later." Rachel couldn't stop herself. "What's his fault?" she asked in regard to Velma's previous quip about Kane.

"Old Charlie's death. Shouldn't have happened."

Rachel checked herself from delving deeper. Was the woman really talking about something that had happened years ago? Anything Velma said might be only gossip, old gossip, she decided.

"You should know the truth. People hold Charlie's death against him. They—" Velma's voice died as she looked past her.

With an askance glance, Rachel saw Kane's truck. She swung back to tell Velma that she'd talk with her tomorrow. The woman was gone, scurrying down the path toward the town square.

Rachel wished she could ignore the woman's words, but they bothered her. She waited on the porch for Kane while he parked. Loyalty to Marnie had made her want to defend him even though she didn't know the facts.

"Were you warned to keep your distance?" he asked, with his approach up the walk, as if he could tell they'd been talking about him. Gossiping, actually. The stubble of an evening beard toughened his looks. What appeared to be motor oil stained the right side of his navy T-shirt near its hem.

"I told you that I'm not concerned." As a young girl when she'd visited Marnie, she had never shied from Kane because of what others thought about him. She'd kept her distance for fear she would act like a blubbering idiot if he talked to her. Back then, sullen and distant, he'd never bothered with her. If given a choice, he'd probably do that now, too, Rachel thought.

"You're too nice, Rachel." Smoky-gray eyes locked on hers while he climbed the stairs. She felt herself being baited and didn't bite. "You'd say anything to keep from repeating some dire message about the evil Kane Riley."

"Are you boasting?"

The firm line of his mouth twitched as if he was truly tempted to smile. He didn't, and she wondered why he held himself so aloof that he wouldn't give in to such a simple response. "Pick up the baby, and I'll carry that in for you," he said, gesturing toward the carriage.

Rachel was determined to make some headway at a friendlier relationship. "Thank you for emptying the van for me," she said to get the conversation going.

"No problem."

She stayed near, waiting for him to collapse the buggy. "I'll start dinner in a few minutes," she said, though she wasn't sure what they'd eat beyond soup and crackers.

"Not for me."

Rachel stared at his bent head, made a face. She had to get rid of the strain between them. Even a day here with him could seem like an eternity if she didn't. "Let's have coffee, then." She really did have something she needed to say. "We have to talk."

Bent over the carriage, he didn't look up as he collapsed it. "About a salary?"

Sensing he would only join her if he felt an obligation to, she nodded. "Yes, that and something else. Just give me a minute, though." She hurried to the bedroom to change Heather's diaper. She really hadn't given money much thought, but this was a man, like his sister, full of pride, someone who'd insist on taking nothing from anyone. Maybe that was her real goal here. The better she understood him, the easier it would be for her to get through to him about Heather.

Rachel stared down at the little one. Her hair was as dark as her uncle's. "Hello, sweetheart," she murmured while she finished diapering her. Lightly she kissed the sole of one tiny foot before slipping it back into the leg of the pink-and-white sleeper. She was so precious, so special. *She's not yours,* she reminded herself. That was something she couldn't afford to forget. Neither was the promise she'd made to Marnie to keep her baby happy and safe.

The smell of freshly brewed coffee drifted to her by the time she approached the kitchen. She'd thought she would make the coffee. She should have known a loner, a solitary man used to fulfilling his own needs, wouldn't wait for someone else to do something.

"Coffee's poured," he said, though his back was to her.

Rachel waited for him to face her. "How did you know I was near?"

"Lemon." His gaze traveled from her mouth to her hair. "What is it? Your shampoo?"

"My—" Rachel touched her hair. No man had

ever noticed something like that about her. "Yes, it is," she said with a calm she didn't feel.

"Nice."

Her legs nearly buckled from shock. Had he actually said something pleasant to her?

He set the cup on the table, crossed to the window, stared up at the sky as if judging the weather. "I'm not rich. But I could come up with a sensible amount for a salary."

Somewhat recovered, Rachel listened as he offered an amount she viewed as more than generous. "That's fine." Aware that he'd probably resist what she had to say, she brought up her brightest smile. "But there's something else we need to discuss."

When he turned back, she saw that wariness had returned to his eyes. He probably felt deluged by problems.

Rachel knew she was going to give him another one. "I'm not sure it's a good idea to search for Heather's father." To avoid the darkening of his stare, she moved to the counter and scooped formula into two of Heather's bottles. He was silent for so long that she felt compelled to look at him.

"That's not the first time I got the impression you were against looking for him." Surprising her, he moved near her, lounged against the counter. "Why do you say that?"

"Marnie might not have wanted it." That's what bothered her most about his idea. She believed her friend hadn't thought the father was best for Heather. "She told me to find you, to give Heather to you."

"The baby is the father's responsibility."

He's like a brick wall, Rachel decided. She fitted the nipple over the neck of the bottle. Was his resistance personal? When he'd said that, had he been thinking about his own father? According to gossip, Ian Riley had cared more about his next drink than his children. If Kane was letting the past influence him, she'd have a difficult time shaking his belief. "That may be true," she said, hoping to reason with him. "But right now you're the only family Heather has. And why would he be better than you?" She looked away in response to Heather's cry. "I need to get her," she said, already on her way to the doorway.

"Rachel—"

She paused and looked back at him.

"He would be better."

A world of pain came through clearly with those four words. Did he really believe that? Why was he so hard on himself? In the bedroom, she lifted Heather into her arms, then rushed back to the kitchen for the bottle. His mistake was still being there. Rachel persisted. "You think a man who used Marnie and left her would be a better father for Heather?"

A hint of challenge skimmed his voice. "You know that for sure?"

"Well, no, but—" She cupped a hand around Heather's bottle. "Marnie could have revealed the name of her baby's father, but she never had, never indicated she wanted Heather anywhere except with you." Greedily Heather sucked on the nipple. "Marnie had thought you'd be best for Heather."

Under his breath, he muttered something earthy.

''That's what you think. You don't know that for sure.''

Protectively Rachel brought Heather a little closer to her breast. Why was life so complicated for her? ''You've never looked at her,'' she said as he started to step away.

Stilling, he half turned toward her. ''What?''

''The baby. You've never really looked at Heather.'' Rachel removed the bottle and lowered the blanket that curtained Heather's tiny face. Eyes squeezed tight, she pursed her lips in a sucking motion. ''She's dark-haired like Marnie.'' Rachel raised her gaze. ''Like you.''

He was staring. Just staring.

''She really looks like Marnie. She's beautiful, isn't she?''

''Tiny.'' His frown deepened. ''I never saw anything so tiny.'' He reached out, gently touched one of Heather's small, curled hands.

Encouraged by his interest, Rachel asked, ''Do you want to hold her?''

He pulled back, hands up. ''No.'' What sounded like a laugh slipped into his voice. ''No, I don't.''

Chapter Four

Rachel didn't argue. In a second he'd placed as much distance as possible between them. She knew then how hard it might be to convince him to keep his niece.

Frowning, she looked away. A more immediate problem insisted on her attention. Three times her stomach had growled before she'd finished feeding Heather and put her down for a nap.

Unsure what his plans were, she made an announcement as she reentered the kitchen. "I might drive into town, get something to eat." While in the bedroom she'd decided that she'd better act now on any plan to alleviate her hunger before he took off again.

He stopped staring out the window and poured another cup of coffee. "Do it soon. The town closes up early."

"All right." Rachel noticed a calico cat slinking toward a tree. Had Kane been watching it? "I'll go now," she said, starting for the doorway.

He moved quickly, faster than she'd seen anyone else move. One second he was by the counter, the next he blocked her path out of the room. "What do you mean...go?" He stood close, so close that the heat of his breath fanned her face. "Without her?"

With effort, Rachel raised her gaze from his chin, from that sensual mouth set now in a grimly straight line. Nerves fluttered in her stomach like a warning. She sighed silently. Like it or not, she was no more immune to him now than she'd been fifteen years ago. "It's silly to take her out as long as you're home."

"For as much as I know what to do, she could be alone." His eyes narrowed to slits. "Take her with you."

His suggestion was ridiculous. Why should she take Heather outside again when she could be snug in bed? "She's changed. She'll sleep for a while," she assured him. "And I should be back before she wakes up for another bottle." Perhaps, like some men, he was overwhelmed by her smallness. "Don't be afraid of her."

His eyes snapped back to her, drilled her with a deadly look.

Not the right thing to say, Rachel guessed instantly. "I didn't mean to insult you. I—"

"Go!" In an abrupt move, he stepped aside to let her pass. "We'll be fine."

Machismo never failed to amaze her. He would obviously accept the challenge rather than be tagged afraid of someone who weighed less than ten pounds. Rachel veiled her smile. She'd reasoned that if Marnie had chosen him to be her child's guardian, why should she doubt his capability to handle Heather for a short time? "I'll hurry," she said to his back.

She'd hurry. Kane grumbled under his breath. That was small consolation if the baby cried. He noticed a few filled bottles of the white garbage that Rachel had scooped from a can. Earlier he'd caught a whiff of it. It smelled awful, and he wondered how the baby could drink it. Probably because she's too young to protest. He assumed she'd sleep until Rachel came back, unless she pulled a fast one on him and stayed away to give him more time with the baby.

He headed to the living room to turn on a documentary about the Alaskan pipeline. He got as far as one step from it when he heard the wail. Damn, she was so small. He wondered if he could avoid picking her up. He'd never held a baby before. Something akin to panic was yanking at him when he entered the bedroom.

She was beet-red, arms and legs thrashing at the air. Could she hurt herself screaming like that? "Hey, come on. Shh." He had no choice. "Come on, Heather. Give me a break. Oh, damn," he murmured and bent over to pick her up.

Honest to the core about her feelings, Rachel faced them while she was driving through town. She was as attracted to him now as before. Maybe even more so. The realization amazed her. She'd agree to live with him for a while, but had never considered complications or old feelings, never thought his touch would flutter her heart as if she were fifteen again. How crazy this was. Never would she have expected this to happen. So now what? The answer seemed simple. As long as he didn't find out, there would be no problem.

At the edge of town, she found an open fast-food restaurant that took forever to fill her order. Worried because she'd been gone so long, she ate while driving back to Kane's house.

She'd been fretting unnecessarily, she assumed when she returned. The house was quiet, and a quick check in the bedroom relaxed her even more. She tiptoed near Heather. Though awake, arms and legs moving, she seemed enchanted with the black-white-and-red mobile of cartoon characters that Rachel had planned to attach to the crib. Kane had done not only that but had also carried in everything that had been on the porch.

Rachel backed out of the room and began a search for him. She found him at a worn-looking mahogany desk in the smallest room. What now served as his den used to be a playroom, then her mother's sewing room. "I'm back," she announced from the doorway. "Any problems?"

"None," he answered without looking up from a pile of papers.

"Thank you for hanging the mobile and carrying everything in." He looked up but said nothing. Rachel lingered only for another moment. With a shrug at his reticence, she returned to the bedroom. Though it took some rearranging of her things in the dresser drawers, she made room in one of them for Heather's clothes. Holding one of the sleepers, a pink-and-white one with a thin band of lace at the collar and cuffs, Rachel remembered when Marnie had purchased the sleepers, kimonas and receiving blankets. How excited she'd been. Everything had seemed so perfect.

Sometimes she couldn't believe her friend was gone. At any moment she expected to get a phone call, hear her voice. That wouldn't happen. Never again. She closed her eyes as a wave of grief heated her eyes with tears. Afraid the sorrow might tighten its grip on her, she nudged herself into action.

In minutes she felt more in control. She finished placing Heather's clothes in the drawer and changed into nightclothes. It was then she noticed Heather had on a dry diaper, properly secured. Well, well. He'd picked her up.

In her nightgown and a yellow robe, Rachel ambled into the kitchen for a glass of water. The bottle she'd left for an emergency was half-empty. While she was gone, he must have looked into the eyes of his niece that were so like his sister's. In some small way they had to have bonded. Before Kane found Heather's biological father, she hoped he'd change his mind, do what his sister had asked and keep her baby.

"You went to Hamburger Haven, didn't you?"

With the unexpected sound of his voice, Rachel nearly dropped the glass in her hand. "How did you know?'' she asked while her heart thudded against the wall of her chest.

Socks and shoes off, in bare feet, he padded into the room. With his hair mussed, he looked more re-laxed than she'd ever seen him. "The employees don't understand the concept of a fast-food restau-rant."

Rachel started to smile but could barely breathe as slowly his eyes coursed down her body, taking a lengthy view of her. She fingered the tie of the robe, more aware than ever how faded, how practical it must look. "You fed her?" she asked, aware of a nervous crack in her voice.

"She was gnawing on her fist. Wasn't I supposed to?"

"Oh, yes. That's why I left the bottle in case she cried for more. I thought—well, it doesn't matter," she said, uncertain if he'd be insulted by what she'd planned to say."

"You thought I might panic."

"You?" She couldn't help smiling now. "Never."

His brows lowered with a scowl. "What was that? A tease?"

He looked surprised she'd do that. It occurred to her at that moment how he must view her—quiet, dull. Boring? Oh, she hoped not. "I've been told that I'm too serious."

He braced his backside against the counter. "And are you?"

How had they gotten started talking about her? "I'd prefer to think of myself as pensive," she said, poking fun at herself.

His lips tugged slightly with a semblance of a smile. "Introspective, thoughtful?"

"Definitely more flattering."

"Have you also been told you're beautiful?"

Her heart stopped. She knew the phone was ringing, that he'd stepped away. But she was caught up in those words. Had he meant that?

The call was for her, and Kane set down the receiver instead of handing it to her, then turned away. He gave himself a mental kick while he wandered back to the den. He shouldn't have said that, but he couldn't help himself. She was inching her way under his skin. He'd stared at her smile, thinking about her kiss, watched her touch the baby and imagined her caress. Something as simple as a turn of her head had made him want to touch the silky strands. Somehow he needed to do damage control now. If he kept things casual, even distant, between them, possibly he'd keep himself from doing something else dumb.

A step from the den, he remembered a marina bill that he'd left in the living room. He did an about-face. In passing, he caught snippets of her conversation. The caller had been male. He'd wondered who it was, then had heard her say the name Sean before he'd been out of hearing range.

She was still talking to him, teasing him about being gone as much as their sister. There was an airiness, a joy in her voice that made him envy her brother. He'd like to hear her talk to him that way. He'd like a lot more. Not smart thinking, he berated himself. In fact, not thinking about her at all would make more sense.

* * *

"What's he like is what I want to know," Sean questioned.

"Do you remember him?" Rachel spoke low, even though Kane was out of the room.

"He was five years older than me, Rachel. All I remember is that he scared the hell out of me. He always looked as if he'd take a poke at you if you looked at him funny."

She laughed. "He still does."

"I'd hoped that wasn't true."

"Why?"

"Because you thought he was the greatest-looking male in the world."

She shut her eyes for a moment, recalling how he teased her unmercifully. Of course he'd been ten then.

"Unless he's gotten fat or bald or both, don't even try to claim indifference."

Hardly, Rachel mused as an image of Kane's rock-hard forearms, his dark unruly hair flashed into her mind. "No, he hasn't," she said softly.

"I rest my case."

"You win, Counselor." In her brightest and most cheerful voice, she assured her brother she'd be all right, she told him not to worry and recounted her plans to help Kane before she said goodbye. But she honestly couldn't say that she wasn't making a big mistake. She decided that she had to take control of the situation.

During the rest of the evening, she avoided him. Actually she thought that decision was mutual, since he'd holed up in the den. To her way of thinking, keeping her distance from him seemed best. Heat had curled inside her from the softness in his voice when he'd said those words. He could make her want; she'd known in that second.

As she pushed aside the shutter and saw a morning sky heavy with pewter-colored clouds, déjà vu grabbed hold. It was as if she were fifteen again. She could visualize Gillian bouncing into the room with some giddy story about her doll. She could almost hear her mother singing in another room. She imagined she heard her father's and Sean's laughter outside. She smiled and would have stayed in the past for a little while longer, but a squeak, a tiny whimper, stirred her from her reverie.

Angling a look at Heather, she saw her bowed mouth pucker in anticipation of food. She was seconds away from bellowing for her bottle.

Rachel scurried for her clothes, tugged on a blue-and-white-striped pullover and her jeans, and wiggled her feet into tied sneakers. Somehow she warmed the bottle and managed to get back to the room before Heather fully awakened.

"Here you are." Lifting her, she pressed her cheek against Heather's soft one for a moment. How easy it would be to pretend Heather was hers. Sitting in the rocker, Rachel closed her eyes to stop staring at the beautiful, tiny features and stop a yearning for what could never be. She listened to Heather's sucking noises, squeezed her eyes tightly, and for the second time in less than twenty-four hours, emotion closed in on her.

She was overtired. Sleep deprivation made a person

more emotional, she reasoned. She'd be glad when Heather slept through the night. While this early wake-up was okay, the two-in-the-morning bottle wiped her out. Not wanting Heather to wake Kane, who, Rachel had assumed, got up around four-thirty or five, she'd set her alarm for two in the morning to awaken before Heather's cry began, but the baby had rung her own alarm early yesterday.

The distinct squeak of the empty bottle now made her open her eyes. She transferred Heather to her chest and gently patted her back. Softly Rachel hummed while she waited for her burp.

She'd assumed Kane had left for the dock before sunrise, and anything she'd want to discuss with him would have to wait until evening. She wished she'd talked to him about groceries. Without some in the house, she'd have to dash for greasy hamburgers and fries every night.

Heather's robust belch stirred her smile. She tucked her into bed and wandered to the kitchen. With nothing necessary to do, and time to herself, she set out to satisfy her curiosity about the one room she hadn't been to—the attic.

She took the flashlight that Kane had hanging near the back door, then entered Sean's old room and unfolded the attic ladder. She climbed it to lift the hatch.

The overcast sky offered only faint light through the attic's lone window. She passed the beam of the flashlight over the boards and rafters of the pitched-ceiling room. Cobwebs draped everything. It appeared that no one had bothered with it since her family had left.

In a corner she spotted a child's lamp with a small, stuffed teddy bear at its base. Her sister had had it in their bedroom. An old Royal typewriter; a lumpy-looking, flower-patterned chair in reds and pinks; and an old-time Singer sewing machine occupied one corner. Nearby was a scarred chest of drawers in mahogany, a worn-looking brass headboard, a four-shelf bookcase filled with dusty books. On the floor beneath the window was a small steamer trunk, its leather straps frayed or broken.

Rachel picked up the lamp. With a cleaning and a new lamp shade, it could be used in Heather's room. But where would that be? she wondered. Not knowing bothered her most. She set the lamp by the ladder and wandered to the chest of drawers. She wanted to see Heather situated somewhere before she left her, but if Heather went with her biological father that wouldn't happen. The man would come and take her. Rachel would never see Heather's room or her home or the backyard she would play in.

Rachel opened one drawer, then another. All three were empty. She scanned the room again, looking for a doll her sister insisted that she'd left in the attic years ago. Perhaps the doll was in the trunk. She'd love to find it, see the look on her sister's face when she gave it to her.

She knelt by the trunk, brushed away cobwebs, then lifted the lid. Sean's first baseball cap with the word Tigers written across the front above the bill lay on top of a neatly folded, worn-looking, yellow blanket that Gillian had dragged everywhere as a toddler.

Oh, Mama. This was theirs. Treasures of the heart

were here. She remembered now how upset her mother had been with the movers because they'd lost the trunk.

She held Sean's cap, recalled the joy on her brother's face when he'd caught his first baseball in a game. They'd all cheered until they were hoarse and their hands stung.

She placed the blanket and the cap on her lap, stared for a long moment at a photograph of her great-grandparents on their wedding day. Her great-grandmother was dressed in a soft-colored dress with a lace collar. She wore a string of pearls, held a bouquet of white gardenias. They matched the one flower in her great-grandfather's lapel.

Rachel put the photo aside, smiled at the sight of a bright-fuchsia boa wrap. Her sister often wore it with their mother's heels and sashayed through the house.

Beneath the wrap were several faded red books. Rachel touched the top of one book. They were her mother's journals. Nightly, for years, she wrote in one. Interested, Rachel opened to a back page of the top book, and skimmed her mother's neat handwriting.

December 8
How lovely Rachel looked this evening. She was so excited about going to her very first dance. She's still a young girl on the brink of womanhood. So soon they grow up. I can't believe how quickly time passed, but then I lost nearly a year, didn't I? Almost a whole year never existed for

me. Time wasted. Oh, if only—no, I must stop now. It will do no good to wish for what can't be changed. Instead I must treasure every moment I do have.

Like tonight. The dress was a perfect shade of green for Rachel. It brought out the red in her hair, made her eyes look greener, showed off her blossoming figure.

More boys would notice her. One already had. Kane Riley watches her. Rachel is not aware of his interest. Just as well. She has a crush on him. As long as neither of them realizes what the other feels, this—puppy love—will not be a problem.

All in all, it was a lovely evening. The school gymnasium had been decorated for the Christmas dance. Red and green streamers hung along the ceiling, an artificial tree sat in a corner of the room. It was lovely, big, shining with lights, decorated with holly and giant-size ornaments, tinsel and an angel on top.

Along with Alan, I chaperoned. We even danced. Tomorrow at breakfast, I'll talk to him about doing this again. I had so much fun.

Rachel clutched the book against her chest. It was as if her mother was near, talking to her. She remembered that dance. She'd just turned fifteen. She'd gone with Chad Olson. She'd been giddy with delight, feeling like a grown-up because he was driving his family's sedan. On the way, they'd passed Kane. He'd been sitting on the dock, just staring out at the night

sky. Was her mother right? Had Kane been interested
in her?

Holding on to the journal, she descended the attic
ladder with it and the lamp. She set the lamp on an
end table in the living room. Eager to read more, she
curled up on the sofa.

Years sped by as she read her mother's entries
about special moments in their lives. A trip to Dis-
neyland occupied a week's worth of entries. Every
special moment in her children's lives was mentioned—Gillian's ballet recital and Sean winning first
place in a science fair and Rachel's first ski lesson.

The book in her hand contained days from the last
three years that they'd lived at the house.

January 11
The plans for our move have begun. I wish we
could stay here. Hubbard Bay is my home now.
I'd begun to think we'd never leave this house.
Of course, I knew Alan's teaching job might
force this move, but I'd hoped we'd stay.

We are fortunate that Charlie is willing to buy
his home back. The dear man. We might have
had a terrible time trying to sell now. But Alan
has to take this job. It's a wonderful opportunity
for him. I hope we like Texas.

Rachel smiled. Her mother had loved her new
home, a lovely ranch with a huge backyard. She'd
had an enormous flower garden that blossomed all
year round.

They'd had some wonderful memories there, and

here. Rachel closed the book. She'd been luckier than some, she thought, recalling how miserable Marnie's and Kane's childhoods had been.

She set down the journal. It had been filled with days from her twelfth to fifteenth year. She wondered if the journals that she'd left in the trunk contained entries of previous years.

She stirred, planning to go back to the attic, when she heard the click of the door behind her. Kane was dressed in a black T-shirt and jeans. His hair was tousled, windblown. The salty smell of the ocean came in with him. She gave him an uncertain smile, unsure of his mood since he'd come home far too early. "I didn't expect you home yet."

Head bowed, he wiped his feet on the mat near the door. "Did you need money to go shopping?"

She rounded a look at him. He'd better be careful. His mask was slipping. Too much thoughtfulness and she'd see past it. "I haven't gone yet, but I won't need money," she said with a shake of her head.

His eyes shifted to the book on the table. "What were you doing?"

"Reliving the past." She held up the journal. "I was reading my mother's diary." Rachel set it in her lap. "I found it in the attic. I hope you don't mind that I went up there. I thought I might find an old doll my sister claimed for years that she'd left up there."

"Did you find it?"

"No, but I found this in a family trunk." Gently she stroked a finger across the top of the diary. It was valuable, precious—to her.

He leaned his backside against a table. "Learn any deep, dark secrets?"

She laughed at the idea. "That's unlikely." Her family had been happy. "No highwaymen or pirates," she said on a laugh but didn't bother to say more. She thought it might be a waste of breath to argue, since she'd heard an edgy quality, something akin to cynicism, in his voice. "There are a lot of things up there."

"Yeah, I know. Charlie's discards. Your mother's too, it seems."

Rachel shook her head adamantly. "I know that she wouldn't have wanted to leave the trunk. In fact, she thought the movers lost it. But there might be some valuable things up there. You're the owner now, you might want to go through it all."

"That stuff is unimportant to me."

Rachel didn't bother to argue. There were people who believed only in the present. He obviously was one of them, and what was in the attic was part of the past.

"You're the talk of the town this morning."

"Me?"

"According to my deckhand, they're saying you're Saint Rachel, that you sacrificed for your sister and brother."

She frowned, didn't know what to say. Sacrifice hardly described what she'd done. "That's not really true." She felt defensive and didn't know why. "We were alone with no one else to care about us. It was such a shock when our parents died. It was a New Year's Eve car accident. They were there, and then they weren't. Sean was sixteen, Gillian was eleven. We all needed each other. We helped each other get through that.''

He dropped to a nearby ottoman, bent forward to rest his forearms on his thighs. ''Tough time?''

''Terrible.'' Rachel dodged a memory starting to form of Sean, Gillian and her at the hospital. ''You asked before if the storm bothers me.'' She made eye contact with him. ''It stirs bad memories. The night they died it was stormy.'' She supposed that sounded ridiculous to him, but storms triggered sad memories for her. ''Do you remember my brother and sister?''

''Not at all.

''I'm not surprised. You must have been seventeen when we left here. They were younger. You wouldn't have bothered with them.'' She felt such pride for both of them. ''Sean's twenty-eight and Gillian is twenty-three. He's a lawyer. In Boston.'' Her brother had worked incredibly hard. ''He's smart, strong-willed and annoyingly independent. You'd understand him.'' Amusement flickered within her at his scowl over her jibe. ''He earned scholarships, worked to pay his way. It wasn't a sacrifice to take care of my sister and brother. They're a part of me, a part of the family I've always known and loved.''

''But you did support them,'' he said, rather than asked.

Rachel untucked her legs. ''You should understand. You took care of Marnie, too.''

''Not long enough.''

Rachel hadn't meant to hit a raw spot.

Head bent, he stared at his hands for a moment,

then looked up. "Why did you move away from here?"

"Because of my father's job. He was a teacher and was offered a wonderful position in administration by an old friend of his."

A flicker of curiosity flashed in his eyes. "It's weird that Marnie ended up in Texas."

"That might be my doing," Rachel admitted. "After we moved, I wrote to her, told her how different Texas was, how much I liked it."

"I wondered why she went there. Did she contact you?"

"I think she knew where I lived and moved near there, and that's why I ran in to her."

A slip of a smile hiked up one corner of his lips. "Don't believe in coincidences?"

"Not really."

"Too sensible for such thinking, aren't you, Rachel Quinn?"

She slitted her eyes at him. "Are you making fun of me?"

"Not me."

The sound of amusement accompanied his words. Rachel had no problem with a laugh at her expense. This time she actually welcomed it because he so rarely let himself laugh or smile. A change swept over his face when he did, softened his features, gentled his eyes.

"So no skeletons in the closet?" he asked, pointing at the diary.

"I don't believe there are any."

"Never know."

She thought the idea ridiculous. Her parents had been so open, so trusting. The only dark moment had been when Rachel was eight, when her mother had been ill. Rachel recalled tightly holding Sean's tiny hand. At five, he'd only known that he missed Mommy. He hadn't understood what their father was saying.

"Your mother is sick and has gone to a hospital to get better."

Rachel had wanted to cry, but she hadn't wanted to scare Sean.

"I'll need you to help me until your mommy gets back, Rachel," her father had said. He'd stood, touched the top of her head before lifting Sean into his arms. "She'll be home soon," he'd assured her, and had draped his other arm around her shoulder to draw her close.

Only, their mother hadn't been home soon. Almost a year had passed before she'd come back.

"You got quiet. Is something wrong?" His movement made her look up. He was standing now, reaching into the back pocket of his jeans.

"No. I was thinking about a time when I was little."

He held a worn-looking wallet. "I'll give you some money. If the groceries cost more, let me know."

Rachel wasn't surprised that he hadn't asked her more about her past. A solitary man would respect another person's privacy. "What shall I get? What do you like to eat?"

"You don't have to bother with me."

"It's silly not to eat together. We're living together." It amazed her how easily those words flowed off her tongue.

He sent her a wry grin. "You never expected to say that, did you?"

Rachel returned a smile. "Never." She stood, planning to protest the money he was about to drop on the table. Reaching out, she grabbed his forearm, stepped forward as he swung back. Their bodies nearly brushing, they stood so near that only inches separated them. Her heart beat faster. What if her mother had been right? Had he noticed her back then?

Youthful fantasies were a breath away from mingling with reality. Rachel stared at his mouth. Would it be gentle or hard? Would it coax or demand? Would it be a mistake to kiss him? What if she coiled her arms around his neck. "I had a crush on you." The second the words were out she wanted to bite her tongue off. Oh, Lord, why had she said that? Heat rushing her face, she gave a half laugh, not believing she'd admitted that to him. This was not a good way to start their time together. They'd be close often, see each other early in the morning, late at night. She didn't need him thinking she expected to be in his bed. "I meant—"

"I know."

Mentally Rachel groaned. Of course he'd known. She'd acted like a dreamy-eyed imbecile whenever he'd been near. Years ago this man had been the first one to touch her heart, to make the girl she was lose herself in dreamy thoughts of him, to stir womanly desire within her young body.

"I thought about you, too." Almost absently he

fingered strands of hair near her cheek, seemed to draw nearer.

She caught her breath. She thought it impossible for her heart to beat harder, but it banged in her chest with his admittance. "You thought about me?"

His eyes, guarded now, released their hold on her own as he let the strands slip through his fingers. "Is that so hard to believe?"

She wanted him to tell her more. "I didn't think— I didn't think you even knew I was alive."

He smiled then, not a stingy one, but one that bracketed his mouth with deep grooves. "I knew."

He knew. She stared after him. Had he really had feelings for her? Oh, what did that matter? She wasn't that innocent teenager anymore. She'd loved and had lost. She didn't want needs aroused again. She didn't want more than she had, or to need anyone but her sister and brother. Mostly she didn't want to open her heart again.

Chapter Five

Rachel was in no mood for Velma but could hardly avoid her if she wanted to shop at the Grocery Mart in town. As she expected, she didn't escape through checkout without another warning from Velma. She eyed the two steaks on the conveyor and shared her opinion. "You should listen to people, not get mixed up with Kane Riley."

People meant her, Rachel assumed.

"I know you girls—" She paused as she ran the scanner over a package of three pork chops. "You girls think Kane Riley is—"

"Gorgeous," a feminine voice said behind Rachel.

The familiarity of it swung Rachel around. Pleasure rushed her as she stared at the face of a childhood friend. "Lori!"

Like children they hugged and danced in place.

Drawing back first, Rachel met Lori Wolkins's deep-brown eyes. They sparkled despite her reprimand. "You said you'd call when you got here."

Rachel offered an apologetic look. "I'd planned to, but I got sidetracked."

A petite blonde, Lori grinned, not really looking upset, and bent over the grocery cart where Rachel had placed Heather's infant seat. Over the phone, before Rachel had left Texas, they'd shared a good cry about Marnie. Now, in the bright of day, she smiled with delight at Heather. "Oh, Rachel, she's beautiful," she said about Heather. "Looking at her could convince me to have one," she said airily. "I'm really surprised you don't have four of your own. You always loved children."

"Plans change," Rachel responded, but her friend was right. She loved being around children. Lori's eyes held hers for only a second, then shifted to an inquisitive-looking Velma.

"Finish with the groceries," Lori urged, "then we'll go somewhere to talk."

Rachel would like that. Besides playing catch-up, she needed information about Kane. She knew she wasn't being objective about him. Because of personal feelings toward him, she believed he'd be best for Heather, but lingering in the back of her mind was Velma's previous words about him and Charlie. How could it be Kane's fault that Charlie had died?

She paid her bill, then preceded Lori outside. "I need to go to the house with these," she said when they reached the van. She set the grocery bags inside, then Heather's infant seat. "Follow me. I have macaroons."

Lori moaned. "Not fair. You know I'll follow you anywhere for them."

At the house, while Rachel unpacked groceries, they discussed mutual acquaintances. Lori made herself at home and set up the coffeepot. "Velma was giving you a hard time about Kane, wasn't she?"

Rachel balled an empty, plastic grocery bag. "I ignore her."

In an interested more than nosy manner, Lori cast a look around at the clean but stark white kitchen. "Remember how nervous you used to get around Kane. Not that I blame you. He always was gorgeous in that quiet, brooding way. Every girl in class thought so, but he was *too* quiet." Lori palmed a head of lettuce and held it out to Rachel. "And now you're…living with him?"

"Lori, I'm not living with him—exactly. I'm here because the baby needs me." Rachel opened the refrigerator door and placed the lettuce in the vegetable crisper. She finished storing perishables, then joined Lori at the table and explained the unique but temporary situation. "I need you to tell me why everyone acts as if he's done something despicable."

"That's easy to answer. Kane was Charlie's deckhand. One night we had a terrible storm, and Charlie was alone on his boat because Kane wasn't there."

"What happened?" Rachel asked.

"Charlie was up in age—seventy-three, I think. Anyway he was too old to secure the boat by himself, but he tried. It was too much for him, and he had a heart attack. That's what everyone in town holds against Kane.''

''But that happened years ago. And it's not Kane's fault that Charlie had the heart attack.''

''People here don't forget. Any of them would have helped Charlie that night, but they'd assumed Kane was there to do it, and he hadn't been. Instead he'd gone to Bangor.''

Rachel couldn't believe he'd be that irresponsible. Marnie had told her often enough that her brother had raised her, made sure she had food to eat, clean clothes, even hovered over her about her homework. That wasn't the kind of man who'd leave an old man without help. ''Why?'' Rachel asked.

Lori looked up and paused in stirring the milk in her coffee. ''What?''

''Why was he in Bangor?''

''I don't know. I'm not sure anyone does.''

The sweet aroma of onions frying hit Kane the moment he stepped into the kitchen later that night. That was the first time he'd opened the door to the smell of food cooking. Her back to him, she stood by the stove.

He roamed into the room and peered over Rachel's shoulder. Pork chops sizzled in one pan while the mixture of sliced potatoes, onions and bacon—he guessed by the smell—were frying in another pan.

He'd told her not to bother. He should have known she wouldn't listen, that despite his protest she would cook him dinner. She was a nurturer, used to taking care of others. For that reason, he doubted she understood his refusal to keep the baby. Yet she'd never really challenged him. Another woman would have called him irresponsible, unfeeling for turning his back on a helpless infant. Though she'd told him she thought he should keep the baby, she'd never made him feel guilty for refusing. He wished she had. He would have been less attracted to her then. She wouldn't slip into his thoughts so much.

He knew it would be dumb to start anything with her. She was the kind of woman who'd assume a commitment went hand in hand with sex, and he wanted nothing beyond a fleeting moment or two. That's why he had no right thinking about her on any level but a business one. The problem was he was having a damn hard time getting her out of his mind.

From across the room he stared into an opened cupboard. Chocolate-covered doughnuts. Spice drops. Potato chips. Kane grinned. The very sensible lady was a junk food addict. The pantry shelves were almost full with canned and packaged food. He'd never had so much food in the cupboards. "Smells good," he said to her back to get her attention and not spook her.

Still she gave a little jump, then laughed. "I didn't hear you come in. You do that all the time to me, you know."

"You should lock the door when alone." Though she'd smiled, what he interpreted as uneasiness clouded her eyes. Was she fretting about what happened earlier? He couldn't make this easier for her. He was having enough trouble fighting himself. Something as simple as a smile turned his thoughts to kissing her, made him want to inch up against her, feel her softness against him. An impulsive man might do that. He wasn't one.

To clear thoughts of her, he migrated to the refrigerator on the pretense of wanting a drink. He checked out its contents. She'd bought a gallon of orange juice, something he enjoyed but usually forgot because he only dashed in and out of the Grocery Mart when necessary, avoiding it as if it contained the plague. For him it did, in the form of the gabby Velma Monroe, whose gossip about him proved contagious to anyone inclined to listen. He wondered if she'd given Rachel an earful. How much of what she'd heard did she believe about him? What did it matter? He'd never worried before about what others thought of him.

Inquisitive, he opened the freezer door. It held at least a week's worth of meat. He closed the door and looked around for the grocery receipt. He spotted it on the far end of the counter. He noted, too, the two cups on the drainboard. She'd had a visitor.

"I hope what I bought is all right with you."

Though he'd given her money earlier, after he glimpsed the store receipt, he dug more bills out of his wallet to make up the difference and set them on the counter beside the receipt.

"Kane, you really don't have to—"

He leveled a sharp look at her. She could protest until doomsday. "I didn't expect you to cook for me. The least I can do is pay for the food."

She sighed as if exasperated, but he noticed a slim

smile curling the edges of her lips. ''You are a stubborn man.''

''When I need to be.'' He hated being obligated. To this day, he recalled the humiliation he'd felt when a social worker had come to their door armed with secondhand clothes for Marnie and him. Some busybody teacher had noticed the holes in his jeans, the tear in his sister's blouse. He'd wanted no part of the clothes they'd been given. And he'd vowed then that he'd always pay his way, never be obligated to anyone.

''I had company today. Lori. Lori Wolken,'' she said, obviously having seen his earlier glance at the sink. ''I know this is your home but—''

''You can have anyone over that you want,'' he said. Though he hoarded his privacy, he had to be generous. The woman was doing him a favor.

''Thank you.''

He caught another whiff of the fried potatoes as she turned away to remove a frying pan from a burner. In anticipation his stomach churned. At the sink he washed his hands, noticed the book on the counter that she'd said was her mother's diary. He wondered why a person felt a need to write down their thoughts. ''Still reading it?''

She looked up from sliding pork chops on plates, her eyes brighter with her smile. All the while she'd been talking, he'd been waiting to see it again. ''I'm having so much fun reading it. I'm going to go back up to the attic for the other books.''

Water rushed over his soaped hands. He honestly couldn't understand her fascination with the past. He believed in now. The past held nothing for him. "What's so interesting?"

"Everything." She placed a spoon in a bowl of corn, lifted the potatoes from the frying pan to a plate. "I read one sentence and a whole day will come to mind. There's so much of our lives in these journals."

While he dried his hands on a paper towel, he faced her. When he was alone again, would he stand here and see her moving around his kitchen? Damn, he needed to be careful, or he'd let his mind play a game of what if she'd stayed, if they'd dated, fallen in love. What if this was his life with her?

"Do you remember Lori?"

Kane pulled away from private thoughts and accepted the plate she held out to him. He waited for her to sit, then took a chair opposite her. He wasn't big on salads, but he figured he couldn't refuse when she offered him the salad bowl. When he was alone, he ate whatever could be cooked in one pan. He did without a plate, serving bowls, and usually ate from the pan. He kept his life simple. Or at least he used to. "I remember her. You three were like triplets."

Her smile came quickly. "We did carry it to the extreme," she said on a laugh at herself. Even her laugh charged up juices within him. "Actually there were four of us," she went on. "There was a girl named Tracy. All of us dressed alike."

"That couldn't have been easy," he responded, trying to concentrate on her words and not get sucked into some fantasy. "My sister's wardrobe was small." He recalled how she'd anguished over that. He hadn't understood why clothes were so important.

"That didn't matter to us. She was our friend." She poked a fork into a salad greens but paused in bringing it to her mouth. "Why did you stop eating? Is something wrong?"

A decades-old memory. The pork was tender, carried a hint of some spice that reminded Kane of his mother's stuffing at Thanksgiving. "Nothing." For years he hadn't allowed himself to think about his mother. There had been too much sorrow. It had finally passed, he realized, allowing his mind's eye to see her, remember how she'd looked, how soft her touch had been.

"I liked Charlie," Rachel murmured between bites. "He used to show me seashells he'd collected. You really got close to him, didn't you?"

Kane figured she'd talk nonstop until he responded. "He had no family. When he died, he left me his boat and the cottage."

She kept eating, seemed content with his answer, but Kane doubted that would be the extent of their conversation.

She proved predictable. "Did you see that movie about the big storm?"

Kane shook his head in answer to her question. Hurting her feelings didn't appeal to him, but he'd never been big on small talk. That didn't mean he wouldn't like to know a lot more about all the years she'd been away. Who had she loved, had some man ever won her heart, caressed her flesh? Did she still like old musicals, peanut-butter-and-jelly sandwiches, crab cakes, the color green? He'd picked his sister's brain one night about her friend and had promised to drop her toothbrush in the toilet if she told.

"What about music? I notice you never have the radio on."

"It's there when I need the weather station." He looked up from his plate and would swear she'd been smiling. "What amused you?"

"Most people listen to the radio for music. I'd forgotten how much of a necessity the radio is to the lobstermen and anyone else who makes their living on the ocean. Did you always want to or was it a chance meeting with Charlie that got you here?"

He was quiet for so long that Rachel thought he planned to ignore her. She'd been worried that there might be an uncomfortableness between them, but except for a few strained moments, they'd been sharing a pleasant meal together—until she'd mentioned Charlie. She didn't want to ruin the meal with questions about him that might anger Kane or make him defensive. And even though she'd like to hear his side of the story, she didn't think this was the right moment. But she couldn't see a problem in talking about his good times with Charlie.

"I always knew I'd live by the water," he finally answered. "But I don't know what I would have been doing if I hadn't met Charlie. I was going to be eighteen in another month, and I went down to the dock to see if he would keep me on."

"You were already working for him?"

"He'd given me a part-time job, but he needed full-time help. He asked if I wanted to go with him and pick up a boat in Florida. He'd heard about one for sale. I figured he'd hire me permanently if I said yes, so I went with him.''

She nodded. ''I knew that. Marnie had said you'd gone there.''

''What else did she say?''

As his eyes narrowed, Rachel wished for the words back. ''Nothing, really. But I know how much she loved you, missed you.''

''She missed me so much that she never came home.''

She heard the hurt in his voice. ''She really did, Kane.'' She wished for the right words. Marnie had talked often about him with affection and at length about missing him. ''She was proud. You'd understand that. I asked her why she didn't call you when she had trouble.'' Rachel set down her cup, hunched forward. She wanted to touch his hand, but thought he'd jerk away. ''All she ever said was that she didn't want to be a burden to you.'' As his head slowly raised, she saw such sadness in his eyes.

He spoke softly, as if more to himself than her. ''Did she think I was like him?''

Him? Did he mean their father? Had he made them feel as if they were a burden to him? ''She said you were wonderful to her, caring and protective. She told me that all you had was each other, that she loved you.''

''I asked a lot of her when I left.'' He didn't sound offensive now, just sad.

''She told me that you had to go somewhere. That the separation was difficult.''

His tone flat, he leaned back in the chair. ''Charlie

was willing to pay good money. I told Marnie to sit tight, that I'd be back soon, and then we could move out, get a place of our own.''

Rachel stilled, afraid to move even an inch for fear he'd stop talking.

''I don't know if he planned to keep the boat, but after picking it up in Florida, this rich guy contacted Charlie and chartered the boat for a lengthy fishing trip with friends. The money was too good to pass up, so Charlie planned to stay. I had a choice. I could stay with him or come back here and look for a job at the Grocery Mart or some place in town. I stayed.'' Silence hung in the air. He stared with unseeing eyes for a long moment, then blinked, seeming to rouse himself. ''Did she act—did she say he—our father— hit her or something?''

Rachel was quick to respond. ''No. Did you think he might have?''

His frown deepened, but he shook his head. ''Not really. He was so lost in his misery that he didn't even know we existed.''

After witnessing Marnie's unhappiness for years, Rachel wanted to understand. ''Why was he like that? Marnie told me that your father stopped talking. He left the house in the morning, went to work and came home long after she'd gone to bed. Was it because he had a hard time dealing with your mother's death that…?''

''A hard time?'' Sarcasm dripped in his voice. ''He fell apart.'' Across the table his eyes locked on hers. ''He simply called it quits on life.'' The defensive edge had returned. ''What else did Marnie say to you?

Did she tell you that she was angry at me? I called her before leaving on that fishing trip. She wanted me to let her come where I was. That made no sense. Being in Florida was temporary. I was coming back to Maine when the job was over. She didn't care. She said I didn't want her, no one wanted her. Furious, she hung up.''

Rachel picked up the spoon beside her cup. ''And that's when she left?''

''I was gone three months. At first, when I called and got no answer, I thought she was still angry and wouldn't talk. But a week later, after not reaching her, I called Lonnie. He'd worked with me for a month on Charlie's boat. I knew he hadn't left for college yet.'' Kane had never thought Lonnie would. ''He's the one who found out for me that Marnie had left. When I came back I asked the old man where she was. He was drunk, incoherent. He said she'd left him ten years ago. She promised forever and had left him.''

''How sad. He was talking about your mother, wasn't he?''

Eyes gleaming with disgust darted to her. ''What was sad was what he did to us.''

Though she empathized with him, sympathy for his father consumed her. He'd been in great pain. ''He lost the love of his life, Kane.''

''When she died, we lost both of them,'' he said with such quiet anger that a chill slithered up her spine. ''A five-year-old girl wept uncontrollably, and I didn't know how to stop it.''

He couldn't have been more than seven or eight, Rachel realized.

"Our father was useless." As if needing a moment to gather some semblance of calm, he stopped, drained the coffee in his cup. "She needed to be held."

Him, too, Rachel believed.

"Instead he clung to a bottle. He admitted that we reminded him too much of the woman he'd loved and lost. It hurt to look at us."

Rachel gripped her spoon tightly. That kind of hurt never left a person. "You held her." It wasn't a question. She knew this man had left his childhood that day to care for his sister.

"I held her. I held her and hated him for not being there for her. And then years later I wasn't, either." With a few words he revealed the regret and guilt burdening him because of those last angry words with his sister. "She didn't forgive me for leaving," he said simply, quietly.

"Kane, she loved you. I know she did. I'm sure she eventually understood why you left."

His face twisted with anguish. "Did she really?" She'd said the words to comfort. Why was he so pained by them?

He stood, shoving back his chair. "I hope you're wrong."

Rachel moved quickly. Standing, too, she caught his hand. She simply wanted some kind of contact, wished for some way to comfort. "She never blamed you for going." Marnie had cried. She'd missed her brother. But what good would it do to tell him that now?

"You'd never walk away, would you?" For a second his hand held hers, only for a second, then slipped free from her grasp. "Never abandon your brother or sister?"

She'd known love. She'd grown up with it surrounding her. Her sister and brother were a part of her, a part of the family she'd always known and loved. "You didn't abandon her, Kane."

"She thought I did."

Kane believed that. Rachel had given him no solace. If Marnie had understood why he'd left, then she'd known he'd only been thinking of himself or he'd have stuck around for her.

That had been impossible then. He'd needed space from the old man. He'd been dying inside, feeling as if their father would bury him. Every day, every minute, he'd felt the old man's pain as if it were his own. How could he have gone on living with him? And though he'd known Marnie was miserable, too, he'd left. In his eyes, he'd let her down, turned his back on her to live his own life, even if it had been for only a few months.

Outside, Kane wandered toward the edge of the cliff. Beneath a sliver of a moon, he stared at the water, dark and choppy. The view was stark, uncluttered. Similar to the way his life had been. Until Rachel had come along. Something had just happened inside the house.

That he'd said so much to her rang like a warning

in his brain. Why had she gotten so close, so quickly? He never stayed after a night of sex with a woman. Though his relationship hadn't crossed that line with Rachel, he'd done something more intimate. He'd shared his thoughts about Marnie. He couldn't remember ever saying so much to someone at one time. Unwittingly he'd taken a step closer.

He'd let her sweetness touch him *again*. It had years ago, too. Whenever she'd smiled at him, he'd thought about kissing her. He figured then that it would have been nuts. That was still true. Only now she was closer, touchable, tempting.

At dawn he stood in the bedroom and listened to her rattling around in the kitchen. Even before he neared the kitchen, saw the light on, he smelled the brewed coffee, the bacon sizzling in the pan.

In the soft glow of the overhead lights, her hair shone like gold threads. He let his gaze sweep over her slender back, the way the robe snugly followed the curves of her hips. He drew in a sharp breath as she shifted and a slender leg peeked out between the opening of the robe. He enjoyed the view for a moment longer, then cleared his throat, figuring that was the best way not to startle her.

A spatula in her hand, she angled her shoulder toward him and raised her head. "Good morning." She flashed one of those smiles that caused a damn tug on his insides. "I hope you like French toast."

He was tempted to step close, slip his arms around her waist. He wanted to kiss her long and hard, get her out of his system. "You're up early."

"If I don't get up early, I'll miss you." Over her shoulder she delivered another smile. This one was filled with understanding. He imagined she was well liked by a lot of people because she genuinely cared about others. "I know what you're going to say. I don't have to do this. But I do miss cooking for other people. As long as I'm willing, why don't you just let me do it?"

Without doing much of anything, she could tip every certainty in his life, he realized.

"Breakfast is ready." She placed plates with French toast on the table. She'd cut the bread diagonally and had dusted them with powder sugar. "Do you have tours today?"

He straddled a chair, realized how much he was looking forward to eating the breakfast. "Lonnie— my deckhand—is taking two fishermen out this morning on the *Maggie Lee*. I'm driving to Portland to pick up a part."

"Oh, really? I haven't been there in ages." A thoughtful expression settled over her face. "Would you mind if we go along."

"Would I...?" He held his fork in midair. He'd been distracted, he realized. All he'd been thinking about was the snug fit of the robe, the way the cloth caressed her breasts and hips. "You want to go with me to Portland?" he asked, trying to zero in on what she was saying to him.

"Yes. I haven't been there in years." As she reached for the syrup, the opening of the robe bellowed to offer him a teasing view of the shadowed vee between her breasts. ''Do you mind?'' she asked between bites.

Mind? He knew what to say, but nothing was easy for him when he was around her. ''If you want,'' he heard himself answer.

Chapter Six

Alone, waiting while Kane went into a small shack near the pier, Rachel wished she could spend the day exploring. Nearly two decades had passed since she'd been in Portland. During one trip, her family had spent the day like sight-seers. She recalled looking at the historic buildings done in a Federal-style architecture, the oldest church, the first cemetery. She'd have liked to go to the public market again and buy produce or flowers, or see the bronze statue of Longfellow.

She'd also like to get something to eat. With her stomach rolling, she surveyed the area for a restaurant or diner. Her eyes skipped over a concession stand that advertised catfish in a basket. But assuming Kane would be anxious to return home and fix his boat, she doubted she'd get a chance to choose somewhere else.

Turning to see if he was coming out yet, she found him only steps from her now. In sunlight his eyes looked darker, his hair glistened a deep, rich black. "That was quick," she said, making herself angle away to check on Heather and put a few more inches between them. With a purpose in mind, she'd invited herself. She'd reasoned that he needed to get used to being around Heather more. Every chance she had, she planned to push them together.

Squinting, he raised a hand to shield his eyes from the glare, and as if checking what boats were gone from port, he studied the ones in the distance for a long moment. In his other hand he held a small box that she assumed contained a new boat part. "I should have told you it wouldn't take long."

So ended her hope of a relaxing day here. Still she knew her stomach would never survive the trip back to Hubbard Bay. "Aren't you hungry? There's a place over there." She pointed, hoped he was agreeable. "We could grab one of those baskets and eat in the truck on the way back."

He glanced at the food stand and grimaced. "Wouldn't you rather have something else?"

Thank you, thank you. "Well, yes, but I thought you'd be in a hurry to go home."

"Not that much of a hurry."

To her surprise he steered her toward a quaint restaurant with a nautical motif and a wonderful view of the water that offered home-cooked foods and specialized in crab cakes.

The day was definitely turning out better than she'd expected.

After they ate, he even agreed to spend time in town. They meandered along the sidewalk, passed unique shops. A Christmas ornament store, a T-shirt and souvenir shop, a quaint watch and clock shop. She window shopped at one of the art galleries, but she had a purpose, wanting to buy gifts for her brother and sister.

In one store window she spotted an advertisement for a circus. "We came to see the circus one year," she told Kane while they were crossing the street. "We were all so excited. When we came to Portland again, it was because my father had entered the annual chili-cooking contest here."

His look of disbelief made her laugh. "Did he win?"

"Well, no, but we had so much fun." She watched his brows knit and hoped with her bubbling version of a family outing that she hadn't stirred up memories of his own unhappy childhood. "I'd like to get that for my sister," she said to draw him out of his silent mood. For Gillian who loved anything odd, she found a T-shirt with a giant lobster on the front to go along with a stuffed animal, a bright red crab. And for laughs, she bought a clock for her brother who nagged with the best about always being on time.

The trip had also been full of surprises, Rachel reflected. She preceded Kane into the house later, set Heather's infant seat in the living room, then hastened back to the truck. "What can I do to help?" she asked, watching him scoot a huge box off the bed of the truck.

"I can handle this. Hold the door."

This was a cherry wood crib for Heather. She couldn't keep sleeping in a temporary bed, he'd said when they'd passed the baby store. The other box in the truck bed contained a matching dresser. And he'd picked up a changing table, too. While he put the crib together, Rachel climbed the attic ladder to retrieve her mother's other journals, so she could read them when she was done with the first one.

She'd thought about mentioning the obvious to Kane. If Heather wasn't staying, why was he spending so much money on her? But maybe, just maybe, this was his way of accepting Heather in his life. Rachel could only hope so.

Rain kept the *Sea Siren* and the *Maggie Lee* docked the next morning. Kane left after having breakfast with Rachel. She didn't know when he'd return, and though her duties didn't include housekeeping, she dusted, then vacuumed.

In need of clean clothes, she tossed her laundry and Heather's into the washing machine. In the laundry room off the kitchen, she was placing Heather's clothes in the dryer when she heard the back door open and close.

Carrying the basket with her laundered clothes, she entered the kitchen to see Kane pouring a cup of coffee. On the floor beside him was a gallon can of paint. "You're going to paint?" She grimaced at stating the obvious.

"She needs a place of her own while she's here." He reached into a bag on the counter. "I bought this, too." He held a cute wallpaper border with teddy bears. Yesterday Rachel had commented about liking it when they'd passed the wallpaper section in the baby store. She hadn't realized he'd paid attention to her. She noticed now that the soft eggshell-color paint he'd bought perfectly matched the background color of the wallpaper.

Pleasure filled her. She knew better than to make too much of his actions, but wondered how he could deny feeling something for Heather. "I found a lamp in the attic. It has teddy bears on it, too. But it needs to be rewired."

"I'll take care of it."

A man of action and few words, Rachel mused as she stood alone again.

He appeared hours later. Showered, his hair damp, he was dressed in jeans and a clean chambray shirt, he dropped to the blue-and-maroon-plaid chair across from her. If she was hoping for a pleasant conversation, she learned instantly that she was wrong.

"Can you recall the names of the men Marnie was dating?" he asked while he withdrew a small notebook from his shirt pocket.

Rachel felt muscles in her shoulders tense. She'd known it was only a matter of time before he'd discuss this with her, but since he'd been decorating the room for Heather, she'd hoped he would change his mind. "Even if you have the names, how will you contact the men?"

He withdrew a short pencil from his shirt pocket, too. "I'll get a private investigator to look for them."

Irritation came quickly, not so much at him but the situation. Stalling, she searched for a way not to give him the names of the men. She truly believed this was where Marnie had wanted her daughter to be.

Impatience deepened his voice. "You aren't going to fight me on this again, are you?"

He'd sized up the moment accurately. That was exactly what she wanted to do. "She dated a trucker, Lee Corgan, for a while," she said because she could think of no way not to.

"How did she meet him? At the bank?"

"She met him at a class at the local college. We were both taking a night class, art appreciation." Rachel had signed up for two other classes, but had a long way to go for a degree. She'd only completed a few years of college when she'd taken over the job of caring for Sean and Gillian. She'd worked at the bank as a teller, and eventually she'd advanced from that position to a loan officer, and then the bank's financial adviser, but the job wasn't all she'd hoped for. "He was taking a few criminal justice classes," she added.

"What can you tell me about this trucker? Did he drive a big rig?"

"He worked for a local distributor. He wanted to join the police force."

"How long did she see him?"

"Only a couple of times." She watched him jotting down the information she'd given him. Concern darkened his face. Rachel guessed he was wondering if his sister had sex with a man she hardly knew. It was a question Rachel couldn't answer. "There was a man named Mark Weller," she said to avoid questions about her friend's sexual activity. "He worked at a public relations firm near the bank. But I don't know if he's still there. Marnie had said she was sorry to stop seeing him, but he was moving away to New York.''

''So he's in New York,'' he said as if speaking his thought aloud. ''And the third guy?''

''His name was Benjamin Gaffney.''

Pen poised on the paper, he raised his eyes to her. ''Where did he work?''

''I'm not sure.'' She tried to remember conversations with Marnie. ''Wait, I do remember. She said that he was a real estate agent. He worked at one of those custom home subdivisions, was a multimillion-dollar seller.''

''Know the name of the builder?''

Feeling agitated, she stood. ''Lamplight—Lighthouse.'' She shook her head. ''I'm not sure. That's all I remember. And that he was polite, nice. I met him. I liked him. He seemed to care about her, brought her flowers, took her to nice places.'' She shrugged. ''But who knows? If he was the one, he wasn't too caring or he'd have never let her deal with all of that alone.'' She felt compelled to remind him, ''Whoever he is, he'll be a stranger to Heather, Kane.''

''We're all strangers to her.''

No, they weren't. Already Heather had inched her way into their lives, was controlling their every minute. She'd kept Rachel from leaving. For a while she'd forced Kane to consider her well-being above all else.

''Do you think the father might not have known?''

He finished scribbling something on the small note-pad.

"I suppose that's possible." Trapped by those gray eyes, challenging her to be honest with him, she had no choice except to share what she knew. "But I believe he was told. Marnie said that she had."

"And he didn't want the baby?"

"I don't know." By the deepening of his frown, she wondered if he'd slipped into the past. Was he remembering how his own father had ignored them? "It's possible he didn't." She felt such anger for Heather. She was sweet and precious. She deserved everything wonderful.

"How will you find out which one is the father?"

"We'll find out." He pushed to his feet. "You could be wrong. Marnie might not have told him that she was having the baby. She might have said that to you."

His reasoning made sense. "I thought that was possible, too," she admitted. She stared out at the dreary-looking sky. "Marnie would do it because she knew that I would keep urging her to tell him. She might lie to me, tell me that he knew, but he doesn't."

"He deserves to know, Rachel," he said, standing close behind her.

She whipped around. "I know," she returned, sharper than she'd intended. She straightened her back and took a few deep breaths to ease away the anger intensifying within her.

"Rachel, you knew from day one this was what was planned."

She couldn't stop herself. She felt such annoyance

with him, with Heather's father, with the miserable situation that had left a baby without a mother. She supposed some people viewed her as a pushover, but she'd had too much grief and responsibility thrust at her before her twenty-first birthday not to know how to stand up for herself or get what she wanted. And she'd always been inclined to say what was on her mind. "What *you* planned," she said, and pointed a finger at his chest.

An instant later her wrist was caught in the viselike grip of his fingers. Emotion flashed in his eyes. She didn't know him well enough to read it, but expected him to level her with some cutting remark. He said nothing.

One moment she was staring up at him, and the next her vision blurred. Her eyes shut as his mouth closed over hers. Nothing would happen if she didn't want it to, she told herself, but she felt shaky, her legs weak. Pleasure blossomed within her. Sensation curled in her stomach. A soft moan hung in her throat. She'd been so annoyed with him for his narrow vision about Heather that she hadn't been thinking straight for a moment. Now thinking stopped.

She slid her hands from his waist to his back while her tongue responded to his, answered the heat of the kiss. The lips slanted over hers sparked feelings, made her ache. As they enticed and persuaded, she strained against him. She felt annoyance as much as pleasure in the mouth on hers as if he wished he hadn't started this, hadn't wanted this. But as if a choice no longer existed, his mouth twisted across hers, taking a deep taste.

A message filled with seduction and urgency swirled on the air around them. Aching, she curled her fingers into his shirt. She'd dreamed of this, had fantasized about it. It had been so long since she'd felt wanted. She'd thought she'd buried those feelings during the end of another relationship. She'd wanted no man since then. No man until now.

Before she couldn't stop, she tore her mouth from his, but a struggle within herself went on. And what about him? she wondered as he drew back with the same quickness he'd used to pull her against him. "You're sorry?" Her heart pounded in her chest. She shouldn't have asked him, put herself up for rejection, but her pride demanded that she hear him say he was yearning as much for her as she'd been for him.

"For what?" Lightly he stroked a thumb across her wrist, across the spot he had held. Despite the strength of his hand, he hadn't bruised her. "Why should I be sorry. I've been thinking about doing that for years."

Never had she expected to hear such an admittance from him. "Years?"

"I told you I thought about you."

She wanted to close her eyes, frame his face with her hands, take another taste. "Why didn't you say anything then?"

"What should I have said? Rachel Quinn, I want you."

Rachel saw annoyance in his gaze. Did she dare go with the emotions he stirred? Not feeling too sensible at the moment, she took a step away. She took only one more when Heather's cry, a gasping cry, resounded through the rooms. In a panic, Rachel raced down the hall to her.

"What's wrong with her?" Kane was at the doorway by the time Rachel picked her up. "Is she having trouble breathing?"

She was hot, too warm, Rachel thought as she held Heather close. "She sounds stuffed up, as if she's having trouble breathing through her nose. And I think she's running a fever." Worry skittered through her. Heather was too young for over-the-counter medicines, and she had no doctor in town.

"What do you want me to do?"

She'd thought he would assume she should handle this, that he'd leave for the boat. "If you have time, we need a humidifier. Could you go to the store to get one?"

"I'll go. Anything else?"

"I need to call a doctor's directory for the name of a pediatrician who handles emergencies." Reluctantly she lowered Heather to her crib and out of her arms. "Keep an eye on her, please." She'd said the words on the way to the door. A look back revealed that he'd moved closer to the crib. From the hall she heard Heather's whimper. Her steps faltered, but she kept going. It was more important to reach a doctor. Hopefully Heather wouldn't cry continuously while she was gone.

Rachel noted that the crying had stopped about the time she exchanged a greeting with a pediatrician. Her concern lessened with his assurances. She made an appointment, and though she wasn't as alarmed,

Heather's quietness rushed her back to the bedroom. "I have—" Rachel froze in the doorway.

He was sitting in the rocker, holding his niece. "She's hot," he said looking up.

"I know." Rachel came close, though she wished he hadn't noticed her. She would have liked to back away, give them time alone, time to bond.

"Did you talk to a doctor?"

"Yes. He said to cool her off. I have an appointment for her this afternoon."

Heather looked even smaller nestled against his broad chest. "What time is the appointment?"

As he pushed out of the rocker, Rachel stepped near to him so he could give her the baby. "One o'clock."

It was an exchange. Nothing more. But they stood next to each other, shoulders angled toward each other, their bodies close. Breaths mingled, his forearm brushed her breast, the back of his hand warmed her midriff. The memory of a kiss hung in the air.

Smoky-gray eyes locked with hers, then lowered to her lips. "I'll go to the boat and be back in time."

Rachel nodded, breathed. "I was going to use Keller's Pharmacy. Are they still in business?"

"Some things never change."

Including suppressed feelings for her. Kane cursed himself on the way to his truck. He thought about the kiss again, about another. How could he not with her so close? He had no excuse for kissing her. He blamed it on a need to satisfy a curiosity that had begun when they'd been teenagers. But one kiss had only made him want more.

She wasn't here for him, he made himself remember. She wouldn't even be in his life if she hadn't agreed to stay for Heather. Heather. She was so small. God, she'd seemed too hot to him. How high a temperature could someone that young have? Was she in danger?

His concern intensified by the time he pulled into the parking lot adjacent to Keller's Pharmacy. He slammed his truck door and hurried into the pharmacy. Inside, uncertain about what to get, he waited for Paul Keller to finish with a customer, then asked him about humidifiers. The pharmacist was civil, his wife cool.

Kane wasn't there to socialize. He purchased the humidifier and drove faster than he should have back through town. He lucked out, getting home without a speeding ticket.

He opened the front door to the sight of Rachel on the sofa with her legs tucked beneath her. Her head was resting on one of the blue throw pillows. With no makeup on and her hair bunched up under her head, she looked like a romantic heroine from one of those nineteenth-century movies. The shutters were closed, and in the darkened room, her skin appeared pale. Eyes shut, she looked vulnerable, sweet. She looked lovely.

Before he leaned over and kissed her again, he strode to the kitchen to fill the humidifier with water. When he was younger, he'd let himself dream about being with her and had convinced himself that would never happen. Kane Riley didn't deserve someone like Rachel Quinn. She was too soft, to sweet, too much of everything good and pure.

He carried the humidifier back to the living room where Heather was sleeping. Draped over the back of a nearby chair was a blue-and-white afghan Rachel had brought into the house from the van on the first day. Kane reached for the afghan to place over her. Instantly he knew it was a mistake. He bent closer, his arms bracketing her shoulders. What if she could be his—for a little while?

Her lashes fluttered, then her eyes opened. She looked unsettled, confused. Because of the nap or his nearness? Would she respond again if he coaxed another kiss from her? He didn't let himself find out. "She's quiet," he said, straightening and looking at Heather. In her infant seat on the sofa near Rachel, Heather snored softly.

"I sponged her, cooled her off. That quieted her." A small frown lingering, she shifted, angling to her right to press her fingertips to the tiny forehead. "She doesn't seem as warm. I was worried." Standing, she folded the afghan, then draped it over the back of the rocker. "When they're so little, it's scary when they get sick. Babies—"

Kane shot a look at her. He'd swear her voice broke.

She pulled in a deep breath as if laboring for it. "Babies are so fragile."

Was she going to cry? Why? He'd been about to say that she was good with Heather, that she needed babies of her own. Instead he said nothing as a far-away look clouded her eyes.

"They don't all have a chance," she said in the quiet, unemotional way of someone who was simply stating a fact. "My baby didn't."

Chapter Seven

The words, so unexpected, rocked him. *Baby? What baby?* He watched her, waited. For a long moment she simply stared down at Heather with such pain in her eyes. How did a man offer comfort for something like this? Would it do any good? Would she want it?

She shook her head. "It's so long ago, but sometimes it feels like yesterday."

She faced him but stared at the floor. He wished he could see her eyes, tell how fresh her grief was. "When?" That was all he asked.

"When I was in college." She pulled in a breath. "There was a man, *the* man, I thought. Keith Wendlow." A small frown wrinkled her brow as if it hurt to remember. "I was eighteen, in love with him and being in love. My parents weren't pleased when I decided to move in with him, but I've always been so sensible. My father convinced my mother to let me live my life.''

Kane planted his feet, not wanting to make noise or jar her.

''Everything seemed wonderful.'' At a window she opened a shutter. ''I'm sure what happened was exactly what my mother had worried about. I got pregnant. Still we were all thrilled, and Keith and I talked about marriage but decided to wait until after the holidays when he'd finished with school. Then everything went wrong.

''I lost the baby in November. He was nearly full term, but not strong enough. I even held him. And then he was gone.'' The hurt spilled out of her. In a protective move, she crossed her arms across her chest.

''Rachel,'' he spoke quietly. What could he do? The question made no sense. He stepped near to take her hand, but knew he couldn't do anything to ease her pain.

She stiffened, seeming afraid to let any emotion go. ''There were complications.'' Her voice softened, and though steady, it was no more than a whisper. ''I can't get pregnant again, can't have children.'' She pressed fingers to her eyes. ''No more babies. That's not a maybe.'' Her voice wavered then. ''I can't have a child.''

He didn't think she'd said the words for him, but for herself as if she needed a reminder. Life wasn't fair. She was the kind of woman who was meant to be a mother. ''I'm sorry.'' The words seemed inadequate. He offered no more sympathy, didn't think she'd want it. Silent, he gathered her into his arms, brought her close.

For a long moment she stayed in his embrace. Then as if slowly awakening herself, becoming aware of her surroundings, she stirred and looked up at him. The slim smile she gave him didn't reach her eyes. On a deep breath, she stepped free of his arms as though she were determined now to stand alone. "I was devastated back then. In fairness to Keith, he tried to help me get through it, but I had a difficult time accepting the loss of my baby. It was so painful, so overwhelming. I tried to act normal through Christmas, then a few weeks passed and my world totally collapsed."

Squarely she met his stare. "My parents were killed in a New Year's Eve accident. Keith tried to offer comfort, tried to be honorable. He said he was more than willing to still marry me, to take in Sean and Gillian. But how could I ask him to bear the responsibility for a sixteen-year-old boy and an eleven-year-old girl? I just couldn't. So we ended the relationship." She said the words with too much ease to be believable. "You're frowning."

Because he didn't buy her matter-of-fact manner. This woman was all heart. He'd seen how she fretted about Heather. She'd feel deeply.

"I didn't end it because of that," she said, misinterpreting his expression. "It was falling apart while I was still pregnant. If it hadn't been, we'd have survived the loss, the added responsibilities after my parents died. But what we felt for each other had begun to change before that."

Kane had had his pain, but nothing like this. She'd given up a dream, Kane guessed. She'd given up a dream of her own family, her own children. He admired her toughness. She'd shown it more than once to him. As recent as yesterday when she'd challenged him about not wanting Heather.

That wasn't true. If he thought he would be best for Heather, he would keep her. This woman, who possessed such inner strength that she coped with so much loss, should understand. He didn't want to hurt the baby, or her—anyone.

What had made her open the most private part of her life to him? Rachel wondered as she sat in the doctor's office with him later. She'd shared none of that with anyone else. Why him? Why had she told him so much? She had good friends like Lori, and several in Texas, and she'd never shared any of that with them. Maybe it was easier to talk to him, tell him everything because he wouldn't try to empathize, wouldn't weaken her with too much sympathy.

"How is she doing?" he asked low, to keep their conversation private in the crowded waiting room. Nearby a toddler whined. Across the room a woman deftly knitted with pale-blue yarn what looked like a baby's bonnet.

"She feels better," Rachel answered.

"And you?" His eyes sliced to her. There was nothing sensual about the look, yet it touched her deeply. Here was a tenderness that few people saw in him. Here was the gentleness that could reach the place within her that she'd tried so hard to protect.

"I'm okay, too," she said softly, and looked up as the nurse appeared at the opened door to the examination room.

"The doctor will see you now," she announced. She looked baffled about whether to address her or Kane. The woman's confusion stemmed from the name on the patient chart. It wasn't Quinn. It was Heather Riley.

Rachel responded, remembering her from high school. "Thank you, LeeAnn." Standing, she stalled, thinking Kane might explain.

Intentional or not, he said nothing to LeeAnn. Rachel had expected him to remain in the waiting room, but when she hefted the diaper bag, he slipped it off her shoulder. "I'll take it."

Peripherally she observed LeeAnn staring after the three of them before they entered the examination room. Possibly Kane hadn't meant to stir gossip, but it had been fueled. In the woman's mind the baby was Rachel's—and his. Before nightfall, everyone would think the same thing.

With medicine in her and the humidifier on, Heather slept easily that evening. Kane was relieved. He knew if he'd been alone to handle the crisis, he'd have messed up. Nothing in life had prepared him for baby care. The one time he'd been alone with Heather when Rachel had left for the fast-food restaurant had proven how inept he was. He'd thrown away three diapers before getting one secured and had felt awkward and clumsy holding her. She was so delicate, so small, so helpless. *I can't help you. I can't be what*

you need, what anyone needs. He'd whispered the
words to her. They were truthful ones. He'd be of no
use to her, to anyone.

Look what he'd done to Rachel now. Earlier, while
in the doctor's office, he'd let the nosy nurse draw
her own conclusions. Years ago he'd stopped wor-
rying whether or not locals were talking about him.
He didn't give a damn if they were. Eventually they'd
stop, even look foolish, because Heather and Rachel
would be gone. So what did it matter what they said
now? He hoped Rachel understood. He honestly
didn't want to upset her. After all, more than once,
she'd been a lifesaver. If she hadn't agreed to stay
and care for Heather, he'd have been sunk.

He'd thought it was no big deal when he'd asked
her to stay. Now he knew differently. Often enough
he sensed her trying to hold a part of herself from the
baby. She'd tended to Heather's needs, hummed to
her, rocked her. But then, as if sensing she'd held
Heather too long, she would set her down in the crib.
He couldn't blame her for not wanting to get too attached. Long ago he'd secured a protective shell
around himself. He'd learned to shut people out and
not care. But unlike him she would care. And he knew
now why the struggle existed within her.

The loss she'd suffered was like yesterday to her.
She must feel that loss whenever she held Heather.
This wasn't fair to her. He realized how much he was
asking of her every time she cuddled Heather. And
what about when they found the father? She'd have
to let Heather go, come up empty again. Yet even
knowing that, she'd stayed to help him.

Restless, unable to sleep, he padded barefoot from his bedroom and down the short hall toward the kitchen. Outside Rachel's door, he stilled in midstride.

A whimper, nothing more, spun him toward the partially opened door. With Heather's cold, Rachel had kept her close in the room with her.

In the crib, her face squinched and red as a pomegranate, her eyes and fists squeezed tightly, Heather opened her mouth to bellow. Before a wail sang in the air, he dashed to her. "You want something to eat, don't you?" he whispered, lifting her into his arms. When they'd returned from the doctor's, still stuffy, Heather had rejected her bottle. He cradled her in his arm. "Hold tight."

In the kitchen he warmed the bottle that Rachel had ready for the two o'clock feeding. He set Heather against his shoulder and patted her back. She whimpered as if her heart was breaking. "Shh." He paced between the refrigerator and the sink; he rocked her. "Everything will be okay in a few minutes."

He expected her lusty wail in his ear at any moment. Snatching up the warmed bottle, he tested the watery, white liquid on the inside of his wrist. "Here you go." With her curled up in the crook of his arm, he offered the nipple of the bottle. Never in his wildest imaginings would he have expected he'd be doing this. Never.

Gray eyes rounded and stared up at him. Gray eyes so much like his sister's that it pained him to look at them. He saw an innocence in Heather's eyes that had once been in Marnie's. If only Marnie hadn't left, if only he'd stayed, if only she was still alive. Slowly, painfully, a pressure worked its way through his chest and filled it, squeezed.

He had no trouble identifying grief. The emotion had closed in on him when his mother had died. He'd thought he'd never feel it again. He'd narrowed his world to include only his sister and Charlie. He'd known the day would come when Charlie would go, but he'd believed Marnie wouldn't die before him. She was younger. Bright and bold and resilient, she was too young to die.

Too young. Hell, of course, she was too young. Anger, unlike any he'd known before, flashed through him. He wanted her back.

Without warning, his throat closed, and heat intensified in his eyes. He drew his sister's child closer to him and dropped to the closest chair. The pain he had avoided enveloped him now. Dammit, he wanted his sister back.

It never occurred to Rachel how exhausted she was until she awoke to sunshine streaming into the room. How was it possible that she hadn't awakened for Heather's middle-of-the-night bottle? She bolted up and saw that the crib was empty.

She's with Kane, she told herself, but with her heart thundering in her chest, she tossed back the blanket, then tore down the hall to his room.

Relief came immediately. While her heart slowed down to a normal pace, she stared at them in the soft light of morning. Sitting on the edge of the bed, wearing only jeans, he held a sleeping Heather. Rachel thought she hadn't made any noise, but he looked up. "I never heard her cry," she said. He looked so comfortable holding her that Rachel didn't offer to take her from him. "How long have you been like this?"

"Most of the night." Head bent, he kept staring at Heather as if she were a treasure.

Rachel's heart opened a little further. "You should have called me." She noticed that he'd moved the humidifier into his room. Steam flowed up from it. Heather was breathing easier and no longer sounded so congested.

"You looked beat," he said while he absently stroked Heather's soft, dark hair. She lay contently against his chest.

Rachel's heart twisted. With his dark head bent close to Heather's, they looked so right together. Why wouldn't he let himself realize that? "Thank you for taking the 2 a.m. feeding," she said, stepping into the room.

"No problem."

But she had one, she realized, unable to take her eyes off him, off all that smooth, masculine flesh. Unabashedly her gaze traveled over his broad shoulders, then coursed down the strong plane of his stomach, the rippling muscles. In fascination she followed the narrow line of hair that trailed downward, disappearing into the waistband of his faded jeans. *Look elsewhere, Rachel.* She lowered her eyes and fixed them on his bare feet. He even had nice-looking feet. *Oh, Rachel, you are definitely in trouble.*

Without much effort, he sparked desire within her. She really didn't want to feel anything, to hurt again.

Go through another loss, but since the kiss, she'd had a difficult time not thinking about it, once worry for Heather had passed. She watched now as he let Heather's tiny fingers clamp over one of his own. "Do you need to leave for the boat soon?"

"Twenty minutes ago," he said in an amused tone.

Passion could be resisted, but what did she do about what she felt when she saw him like this with Heather? These moments could weaken all her resolve. "I'd better hurry and make breakfast," she said, before she drove herself crazy.

Breakfast was a rushed affair, though he ate the scrambled eggs with gusto.

"I'll be back late," he announced while scooping up the last of them on his plate. He'd already told her that he had a whale watch tour and a sunset fishing trip with three men from Boston. "What are you going to do today?"

Good question, Rachel mused. "I have no idea." Unable to go out because of Heather's cold, after he left, she busied herself in the kitchen, mopped the floor, then baked a loaf of banana bread.

The banana bread was in the oven when Velma stopped by with a bucket of blueberries and a claim that she had too many. Rachel figured Velma was nosing around, trying to see what was going on inside the house. Rachel thanked her. And it was then she decided to make jelly.

Along with her mother's journals, she remembered seeing a recipe book in the trunk. About the size of a man's hand, the cookbook had a well-worn, black leather cover. She retrieved it and a typewriter from the attic. Tomorrow she'd go to town, get a ribbon for it. But today she'd make use of one of the recipes she'd found in the cookbook.

Before Heather awoke for her bottle, Rachel gathered a kettle, double boiler, a kitchen scale, and half a dozen mason jars from the cellar. After sterilizing the glass jars, she washed the blueberries. She crushed them, then put the cooked fruit in a bag made of cheesecloth and hung the bag to let the juice drip into a bowl overnight.

She'd spent the day on her feet, and after bathing and feeding Heather, wise or not, she sat in the rocker with her and remained there long after the baby had fallen asleep. With every breath she took, she drew in Heather's sweet scent, and an ache swept through her, an unsatisfied longing, one she'd begun to realize would never be forgotten.

Later, after putting Heather to bed, she had some time to pass until Kane came home. While keeping an eye on the beef braising in a pot, she reached for one of her mother's journals. She set aside papers that had fallen out of the diary: a school Christmas program when Sean played Scrooge, a Valentine's Day poem from Gillian to her mother. She turned pages to one passage that had made her laugh the first time she'd read it.

December 25
Alan was right. The saxophone was what Sean wanted most for Christmas. Since early this morning he's been playing it.

Rachel closed the book. *Playing it* weren't the words she would have used to describe the off-key blaring notes.

"You're smiling."

She raised her head. Caught up in her own thoughts, she hadn't even heard the sound of Kane's truck. "I was remembering when my brother got his saxophone." She took in the sight of him. His jaw dark with stubble, his hair windblown, he looked tired after a day at sea. He also looked wonderful. His tanned face appeared a shade redder from hours in the sun. "I used to wear my fuzzy blue earmuffs around the house to drown out the noise of him playing and the neighbors's dog howling.

"Blue earmuffs?"

"Fuzzy ones," she said on a laugh.

"What's going on there?" He pointed in the direction of the typewriter and books spread out on the dining room table.

"I need to do something. I'll go crazy sitting around here. So I thought I'd type these old recipes. Maybe get a cookbook published." She supposed that sounded kind of unrealistic, but she'd been carefully turning pages in the recipe book. It was no longer bound, and its pages had turned yellow, but its contents had held her interest for hours.

She recalled seeing it not only in her mother's kitchen, but also her grandmother's. "I noticed that the name of the contributor had been scrawled at the bottom of each recipe. Most of them belonged to my family and were passed down from my great-great-

great-great-grandmother. I think that many greats, maybe more." She'd swear she heard him chuckle.

Though not even touching her, he turned a rarely seen smile on her. With a look, she felt as if she was being caressed. Sensations swarmed in on her. So did the truth. She was yearning to feel the heat of his mouth, the stirring from his kiss, that breathless, dizzy sensation again. She wanted him. She wanted to make love with him, take that chance. What would he say if she pressed herself against him, if she slid her hands beneath his shirt? Can he read my mind, know I'm lusting for him? More than anything, she didn't want him to take her in his arms out of some kind of pity for poor, needy Rachel.

Kane watched her move with a nervous energy away from him and to the stove. He'd told himself that he didn't mind being alone, but ever since she'd shown up at his door, he was having a hard time remembering that. Constantly she aroused a need inside him that he'd thought he'd buried—a need to get close to someone.

"I hope you like pot roast."

As she turned with a platter in her hands, he spotted the rows of mason jars on the counter. Nearby, tiny sprouts in six-inch plastic pots occupied space on the window sill. "What are those?"

"Herbs." A frown etched a faint line between her brows. "I hope you don't mind that I put those there."

"It's fine," he said, but he felt uncomfortable. She was making the house look like a home. "Tomorrow I'll contact someone to search for those men," he said, thinking they both needed a reminder. Nothing that had happened between Rachel and him was meant to go on. He couldn't let one kiss make him think about having things he'd abandoned long ago. "You said that your brother's a lawyer, didn't you?" He tried to steel himself to the plea in her eyes to stop this. "Could he handle that kind of thing?"

"I don't think so, but I'll ask him."

He didn't need to be a mind reader to tell that that phone call wasn't one she wanted to make. Just as deliberately, it seemed, she forced another reminder on both of them. "Have you found anyone for the nanny's job yet?"

He slanted a look her way. He hadn't forgotten she wanted to leave, go home. As she reached for the telephone, he headed for the door to give her privacy. "I called an employment agency," he told her. "They said they'd have applicants call me for an interview." He stepped into the other room, putting distance between them. And swore.

FREE GIFTS!

NO COST! NO OBLIGATION TO BUY!
NO PURCHASE NECESSARY!

PLAY THE
Lucky Key Game

Scratch gold area with a coin.
Then check below to see the gifts you get!

335 SDL DC65
235 SDL DC6Z

YES! I have scratched off the gold area. Please send me the 2 Free books and gift for which I qualify. I understand I am under no obligation to purchase any books, as explained on the back and on the opposite page.

NAME   (PLEASE PRINT CLEARLY)

ADDRESS

APT.#   CITY

STATE/PROV.   ZIP/POSTAL CODE

2 free books plus a mystery gift	1 free book
2 free books	Try Again!

(S-SE-OS-07/01)

The Silhouette Reader Service™ — Here's how it works:

Accepting your 2 free books and gift places you under no obligation to buy anything. You may keep the books and gift and return the shipping statement marked "cancel." If you do not cancel, about a month later we'll send you 6 additional novels and bill you just $3.80 each in the U.S., or $4.21 each in Canada, plus 25¢ shipping & handling per book and applicable taxes if any.* That's the complete price and — compared to cover prices of $4.50 each in the U.S. and $5.25 each in Canada — it's quite a bargain! You may cancel at any time, but if you choose to continue, every month we'll send you 6 more books, which you may either purchase at the discount price or return to us and cancel your subscription.

*Terms and prices subject to change without notice. Sales tax applicable in N.Y. Canadian residents will be charged applicable provincial taxes and GST.

Chapter Eight

Alone, Rachel punched out her brother's phone number. It was probably best for her to go soon. It was getting harder and harder to ignore the desire crackling in the air between her and Kane, to keep herself detached from him and Heather.

Sometimes she was so foolish. She'd hoped—really had hoped that he would change his mind, keep Heather, and she could return to Texas, her conscience free that she'd done as Marnie wanted.

He'd seemed to be enjoying having Heather at the house. Hadn't he painted the room for her, bought her furniture? Oh, what did she know about him really?

A click in her ear snapped her back to the phone call. ''Can you help us find Heather's father or know someone who could?'' she asked after Sean finished a polite third-degree about Marnie and her relationships. She was looking for love, Rachel could have told him in her friend's defense. She was a beautiful woman who had never come to terms with her past, with all she'd yearned for, and in the process, her values got misplaced, needs became materialistic, her life unhappy. "She was important to me." She'd known the sweet girl, the one who loved popcorn, the one who giggled whenever a boy smiled at her, who hero-worshiped her big brother.

"I didn't mean to upset you," Sean said.

"I know." Cradling the phone between her jaw and shoulder, she ambled around the kitchen nervously. "I believe Marnie meant for Heather to be with her brother."

"The biological father has legal rights, not your friend's brother."

She knew that, but still the words fluttered around in her stomach.

After several days of being stuck inside, Rachel wanted to go outside the next morning, take a walk. As if by mutual agreement, she and Kane managed to stay clear of each other through the rest of yesterday and early this morning.

At the stove she finished making the jelly, and stirred up a pot of clam chowder. She gazed out the window, feeling as if she'd go stir-crazy if she didn't get out soon. She yearned to feel the wind in her hair or the spray of the ocean on her face. Kane had left the house at dawn to a sky filled with heavy, pewter gray clouds, but rain hadn't begun yet.

Because she assumed he'd be out for the whole

day, she never expected to look up after turning off
the stove burner and see his truck. It was dumb, but
her heart pounded harder. He wasn't home for her,
she reminded herself. He must be here because...
because—well, she was sure he had a good reason, a
reason that had nothing to do with her. "The fishing
trip was canceled?" she asked when he entered the
kitchen.

"No." He stayed at the doorway, looked a touch
uncertain. "Lonnie's taking them." He had no idea
why he was here, Kane realized. He'd stood on the
boat, thinking about her, remembering how dedicated
she'd been to Heather during her bout with the cold,
and felt she deserved some time away from the house,
from him. Yesterday she'd mentioned a nanny. What
came through clearly was that she wanted to leave,
was anxious to get back to her life. "If she's doing
all right, do you want to go out?"

"Go out?" She laughed in that soft, throaty way
that made his mind shift and think of a hot body—
her—wrapped in his arms. "I'd love to. I was going
stir-crazy. The school fair is on today. That's a lot of
fun, and most tourists don't go."

The school fair? It was a family function, a community event. Something other people, people like
Rachel, went to. "Never went to it." He'd had no
desire to step back into the high school after he'd left
it.

"It's fun. Really. Each class makes a different proj-
ect to display at the fair. There's always music and
plenty of food." At the counter she poured soup into
a container for the refrigerator, then cast a glance at

the stormy-looking sky. "It'll take me a few minutes
to get Heather ready."

He realized she'd assumed all three of them would
go. He'd been thinking he would stay home with
Heather and give her a day to herself. He'd been
thinking how beautiful she looked. He'd been thinking how much he'd like to touch her. "You should
go alone."

She turned, faced him, and it took every ounce of
willpower he possessed not to lean closer and take
her mouth. "You don't want to go?"

"Rachel, I should have never started anything with
you." Even as he said the words, a yearning to feel
her against him made him inch closer. He watched
her lips part. He meant only to take a taste, satisfy a
need to just once more feel her lips beneath his. He
even tried a game in his head, sure that if he kissed
her until her taste no longer interested him he could
walk away from her. An impossibility, he realized as
he twisted his mouth harder across hers.

She made him ache. She awakened feelings he'd
always had control of. He felt the heat rising within
him as he let his hands move over her slimness. He
could think of nothing but holding her, savoring her
sweet taste. He wanted to lose himself in her. It didn't
matter that he wasn't any good for her. He wanted
her. He wanted everything possible with her.

Slowly he lifted his head, stared into eyes soft with
passion, at her lips swollen from his kiss. Lightly as
a feather he brushed her cheek with the back of his
hand. Not just the softness of her flesh, but the softness within her reached out to him. He took a deep

breath, inhaled her scent, wanted to crush her against him again. She deserved so much more than a quick affair.

"Go with me," she murmured breathlessly against his cheek. "Please."

Silently he cursed himself. He couldn't have said no if his life depended on it.

Rachel rushed into the bedroom to change and dress Heather. He'd made her want again, feel alive again. No denial would work, and for a long moment she stood still in the middle of the room, steadying her breaths. Certainly the attraction she felt for him hadn't been in her plans. She'd come to see him because of Heather. But she couldn't pretend this was only about Heather anymore.

"I'll drop you off so you won't get wet," he announced when they neared the high school.

Rachel regarded the back-and-forth movement of the truck wipers as rain fell lightly. He was trying to pull away again. "Drop us off where?"

"At the gym entrance." He made a right turn, then glanced sidelong at her. "I'll meet you inside later."

She wasn't sure where she wanted to go with him, but she knew she didn't want to back up. "Where are you going?"

"I have to stop at the bait shop and talk to Junior Thompson."

She'd learned from Lori that along with the house and the boat, Charlie had left Kane the bait shop. "We could go with you."

He shrugged, appearing indifferent to her request. "If you want."

She didn't know what she wanted. That was the problem. Nothing between them was simple. After fifteen years away from him, she hadn't banished the thrill when he looked at her, or the way her heart beat double-time when he touched her. And now that she knew his kiss, she wasn't sure she could forget it.

With his turn toward the pier, the smell of fish permeated the air. Despite the drizzle, tourists browsed in and out of shops near the dock. Sounds mingled—the bell buoys, the screeching seagulls, the roar and crash of the ocean. Rachel observed a worker on a charter boat casting off.

"I'll be a minute." Kane braked, leaving the engine running, and dashed into a gray and weathered building. Rachel had been inside Charlie's Bait Shop once with her brother Sean. She remembered how the musty odor of fish hit before a person's eyes focused in the interior's dim light. She doubted that had changed. As the shack door opened now, Kane emerged with a fiftyish man. She guessed that was Junior Thompson. The juvenile moniker hardly suited the barrel shaped, balding man. By his robust-sounding laugh and the pat on the back he gave Kane, she assumed he had a congenial nature. "That's Junior?" she asked when Kane returned to the truck.

The man in question had already reentered the bait shop. "That's him. He has a live-and-let-live attitude, which is why he had no trouble being employed by me."

She thought he might be imagining everything. She

found it difficult to believe that everyone in town snubbed Kane.

The moment they entered the gymnasium, she knew she was wrong. The buzz of conversation rose and followed them when Rachel walked beside him down the hall. She wasn't prepared for this, the curious stares, the whispers. Troublemaker. Useless. No-good. She could hear the words and felt bad for Kane, certain he heard them, too.

He'd lived in this town all his life, but Rachel doubted he would say that he belonged. She tried to pretend nothing was happening, but she couldn't ignore the dour expressions, the disapproving glares, the concerned frowns by some, as if they thought she deserved their saddest thoughts.

Growing annoyed at the attitudes of others, she bent over and checked on Heather in her carriage. Contact with the little one always soothed her. She waited for her mood to gentle, then turned her attention on a beautiful patchwork quilt on display. "This is lovely," she told the woman who was beaming with pride about her handiwork.

"Rachel? Rachel Quinn?" A heavy-set woman dressed in a pink flowery dress flashed a bright smile at Rachel before sweeping her into a bear hug. "You are Mary Ann and Alan Quinn's oldest, aren't you?"

Drawing back, Rachel kept a smile on her face and mentally searched for a name.

"Bet you don't remember me. I'm Libby Cosley. I was one of your mother's Thursday bridge buddies."

"Oh, Mrs. Cosley, of course. Hello," Rachel said

with genuine enthusiasm as she recalled the woman who made wonderful pastries. "I loved your cherry tarts and brownies."

"You were such a sweet and polite girl." As her gaze riveted on Kane, her smile faded. "I'd heard you were back in town."

"Only for a visit." Rachel thought of gluing herself to his side, a symbolic gesture to convey that he wasn't alone. He had other ideas.

Scowling, he wandered away to read a bulletin board. Was he angry at her for forcing this outing or at himself for going along with her? Rachel didn't have time to ponder that question. Now that she was alone, she'd become surrounded by Velma and her friend, Dorothy Bensen. Dorothy's attention shifted to her mother. Using a walker, Edith Bensen, a thin and frail-looking woman, inched closer to join them.

"Everyone is talking about you. And *him*." Disapproval oozed from Velma's voice, hung in the air as the other women shook their heads disapprovingly. "Hasn't he done wrong enough by you, Rachel?"

What in the world were they talking about? "Excuse me?"

Pointedly they all looked down at Heather in her carriage. "We heard she was in the doctor's office." LeeAnn always had a runaway mouth. "That the baby's name is Heather Riley."

Rachel had enough of their innuendos. "Yes, it is." She decided it was time to set everyone straight. "The baby is Marnie Riley's. I came to town to bring the baby to Kane."

Instead of ending their looks of censure, their

frowns deepened the lines in their faces. Velma asked with disdain, "She doesn't want it?"

Indignation for her friend bubbled within Rachel. She suppressed it, was glad Kane had moved away, out of hearing. "She died giving birth."

With a blink, sympathy swept over Velma's face. "How terrible. We didn't know."

Dorothy Bensen clucked her tongue. "I'm so sorry, too."

Rachel believed their responses were genuine. "Thank you." She didn't plan to elaborate. All that needed to be promulgated had been said. Before evening that news would spread like wildfire. "I need to leave." She glanced Kane's way. Had he kept his distance to let her socialize or keep her from being the hot topic of gossip?

Velma's sturdy hand clamped on Rachel's arm, stopping her from moving away. "Rachel, Charlie Greer would be here today if it wasn't for him. Please remember that."

Rachel straightened her back. These weren't malicious women, only narrow-minded, Rachel reminded herself. And their feelings about Kane weren't because of meanness. In their minds this was about injustice. They'd lost a dear friend, and no one had paid. Still, annoyance churned within Rachel. Though she didn't know the facts, she knew Kane.

Repeatedly he'd revealed a gentle, caring nature around Heather. He'd shown such sensitivity to her when she'd told him about her baby. The man others had condemned as thoughtless and irresponsible was not the man she'd been living with. "I know that Charlie was everyone's friend, but—"

Briefly Velma spared a look at Kane. "He hasn't changed, Rachel. He still causes trouble."

The woman lumbered away before Rachel could respond. Irritated that she hadn't had her say, she wished to yell at anyone who'd listen that they were wrong. Instead, Rachel's gaze fastened on Kane standing across the room, and she pushed Heather's buggy over behind him. Like him, she studied the huge model train display complete with papier-mâché mountains and tunnels. "It's really nice, isn't it?" She noticed it was the work of eighth-grade students. "They did a great job."

He swiveled a look over his shoulder then. "She gave you an earful about me, didn't she?" he said instead of commenting about the display.

Rachel didn't want to discuss that or let others spoil the day for them. "Let's get something to eat." Minutes ago her stomach had growled, but she'd forgotten about her hunger with Libby Cosley's approach. Now she eyed the hot dog concession stand nearby. "I vote for a hot dog. What do you want?"

He caught her arm, stopped her from pivoting away. "Don't defend me, Rachel. You'll get hurt. People don't forget anything around here." He stared past her, scanned the sea of faces. "And they don't forgive easily."

He released her arm as if to indicate there was nothing more to say, but she had to ask. "Is there something that needs forgiving?"

"Yeah, there is." He spoke low, in a tone edged

with resignation. "I let the old man down. I wasn't there for him. Just like I let my sister down."

She couldn't believe he would do anything to hurt Charlie. Whenever Kane talked about him, affection filled his voice. "I can tell that Charlie meant the world to you."

"He was important," he admitted. He curled his fingers around her upper arm, urged her to walk away from the crowd. "He gave me a chance for more than I ever expected. I owed him big-time. He took in a kid with a lousy home life, gave him a job. He was there for me whenever I needed someone to talk to about having to go to the tavern again and bring home my father." The anger, not at her but himself, intensified, darkened his eyes. "And what did I give him? Nothing. When he needed me most, I wasn't there. That's what everyone in this room knows."

Everyone was wrong. Rachel truly believed that. The night Heather had the fever, Kane had been the one who'd sat up with her. Kane possessed a deep ability to care. That's why guilt about Charlie, about his sister, shadowed him. She looked around her. Everyone in the room was wrong about Kane.

While her mind had mulled over his words, she noticed now that he'd gone for the hot dogs. Rachel sidled close, was surprised that he was having a conversation with the middle-aged, gray-haired man who'd volunteered for the job of hot dog vendor.

"Lou Banning," she heard Kane say, as if confirming the man's words.

"Yep. That's the name. Works out of Portland."

Rachel thought Kane had muttered a curse. "Thanks, George."

That he was actually friendly with the man astonished her. "I don't know him," she said, accepting the hot dog from Kane. It seemed he did have friends in town.

"His name is George Landis. He's new in town, an attorney. He never knew Charlie, so he has no reason to dislike me, but we're not friends. If he was, no one would go to him, and he'd have to yank down his shingle." He handed her a napkin. "Let's go over there," he urged, gesturing with his head to a small table by a wall. "I was asking him for the name of a private investigator."

Rachel's appetite waned.

"I should have taken care of this when we were in Portland, but I was thinking about the boat. I have to get answers."

She hated this. *Keep Heather,* she wanted to yell. "I did talk to my brother. He didn't know any private investigators." She hadn't wanted to call Sean, but if Kane didn't want to keep Heather, there was little she could say to change his mind.

Slowly, so slowly that she felt caressed, his gaze rose from her lips. "I wasn't sure if you'd do it."

Rachel stared at the hot dog overloaded with chopped onions, tried to think clearly. No easy task. Without much effort he kindled warm pleasure within her. "I didn't have any choice. I can't stay away too long," she said firmly. "Or I'll lose my job."

He reached out, snagged her wrist, halting her. "You need to make up your mind, Rachel."

Her head snapped up. "What do you mean?"

"You don't want me to look for Heather's father, but you're telling me you can't stay." A definite challenge edged his voice. "You can't have it both ways."

"I'm not contradicting myself," she returned. "I can't stay much longer. But I can leave without Heather leaving here."

"By leaving her with me?"

"Yes, by leaving her with you," she said softly, aware they'd grabbed the attention of several people as tension radiated through the air between them.

He spoke low, his stare steady. "That's not going to happen, Rachel."

He made nothing easy for her, Rachel decided during the drive home. If he'd agreed to keep Heather, she could leave, and she'd have honored a promise to her friend to be with Heather until Rachel was sure that she was where she'd be happy.

Somehow she still had to convince him how right it was for him to take Heather. She believed his resistance about Heather wasn't because he was selfish or afraid of commitment. More likely his refusal stemmed from dealing with his father's inadequacies, from a belief that a child belonged with its parent. That seemed so illogical, especially for him. He'd grown up with a parent who'd failed to provide his children with love and affection. Firsthand, he'd learned that not all parents were the best people to raise a child.

At the house Rachel put Heather to bed. Kane, silent since they'd left the school, disappeared into his den to work on a balance sheet. Under his breath he'd muttered something about "those damn numbers."

He amused her. It was logical that a man who worked with his hands would hate paperwork. Certain she'd be alone for a while, Rachel checked on a sleeping Heather, then plopped cross-legged on the bed with her mother's journal. The way she'd done with the other diary, she fanned pages. Again slips of paper slid out and onto her lap. She unfolded one. The writing was masculine, the signature her father's. The letter to her mother was dated December 16.

My darling Mary Ann,
I miss you, my darling, and I hope as you read this that you understand the words. I will try to visit next week. I'm so lonely when a week passes, and I don't hold you. Only you fill my heart. I pray you'll be better soon and you'll be home with us.
    With all my love always,

                          Alan

Frowning, Rachel set the folded papers that had fallen out earlier beside her on the bed and thumbed pages to find the December 16 entry. She got as far as a previous, September passage.

Not the words but the shakiness of her mother's handwriting caught her attention.

September 2
I wake up so tired. I'm always tired. Unhappy.
I want to close my eyes. Forget.

Rachel clutched the book. This one contained the years around her eighth birthday when her mother had been ill.

Neighbors had visited them. Rachel recalled one conversation she'd overheard. The words hadn't made sense to her then.

Clinical depression.

No improvement

Shock therapy.

"She doesn't talk or look at me," her father had told the neighbors in a broken voice.

As a child Rachel hadn't fully understood. She'd only known her mother was going to have a baby, and now she wasn't. Later her father had come to Rachel's room, told her that he needed her help. It was then, after her mother's miscarriage, that she'd begun to watch over Sean, that a closeness had begun with her father that had grown.

She'd missed her mother so much. Despite her father's best efforts to keep everything normal, Rachel recalled a sadness clinging to the air during that time. She knew now that her mother had had a nervous breakdown after she'd lost the baby. Ironically she herself had endured the same kind of emptiness that came with such a loss. But her mother hadn't coped. Months had passed before she returned home, before their lives had been normal again.

How fragile her mother had still been when she'd

come home. Rachel picked up another folded paper. She wished when she was older that she'd talked to her father about that time, but everything had been so wonderful after their mother had come back that she'd barely remembered those months when she'd been absent from their lives.

Words her mother had said years later came back to her. The day Rachel had lost her baby, her mother had come to the hospital, had simply held her, let her cry in her arms. "Never will you forget," she'd said. "But the pain will lessen."

Straightening her back, Rachel blinked hard against the tears smarting the back of her eyes. She should go to sleep. What was the point in dwelling over any of that? She held the paper in her hand for a long moment, then unfolded it.

She needed sleep more than she needed—

Everything stopped. Her heart, her breath, her world. She stared at the paper in her hand. Simply stared. She read it once, twice, a third time. It took that many times for the words on the official-looking paper to register in her mind.

"State of Maine, Application for Adoption."

Adoption. Adoption. Who? Who was adopted? One of them? Which one of them? Was it her? Or Sean? Or Gillian? Think. Think hard.

She'd been three when her mother had Sean. She'd pressed her ear to her mother's tummy, listening hard. And Gillian? She couldn't remember her mother's pregnancy that time. Of course she could. No, she couldn't. She recalled that she and Sean had stayed at their aunt Cheryl's for a while. But she couldn't remember if she'd seen her mother pregnant with Gillian, or if the time she was remembering was right before her mother had the miscarriage.

Maybe it wasn't her sister. Maybe *she* was the adopted baby?

Chapter Nine

It didn't matter how late it was. She couldn't have gone to sleep, didn't even try. The most vital fact on the yellowed paper didn't exist—the date. Rachel didn't think anyone had deliberately removed the date. At some moment the top-right corner of the paper had been torn off.

Slowly she stood beside the bed and slipped on her robe and slippers. Uncertain if Kane was sleeping, after she retrieved a flashlight from a kitchen drawer, she moved quietly to the attic ladder. She had to find that torn-off piece of paper. A sick sensation curled in the pit of her stomach. Anger played over her, tensing muscles through her whole body. How could she go her whole life and not know? How could her parents have adopted one of them and never said anything? An omission of truth was a lie. Had they all built a wonderful, happy family on a lie?

She waved the beam of the flashlight around the dark attic. With effort she strove to settle both the fury and unexpected nerves. The wailing wind added an eeriness to the moment. Everything from the outline of a dressmaker's mannequin to a coatrack came alive. "Don't spook yourself," she murmured.

She had something too important to do to scare herself into retreating back down that ladder. But a creak behind her jerked her around. Heart pounding, she directed the light toward the noise. The light aimed at air fell across Kane who was standing on the ladder. His face was illuminated in a surreal glow, only the upper half of his body visible.

"What are you doing up here so late?" he asked while finishing the climb into the attic.

She dragged a hand at her hair, tucked strands behind her ear. "I need to search the trunk." She sent the light over it and crossed the plank flooring.

"The trunk? Why?"

"I need to search it," she repeated, not veiling her annoyance at being bothered. She didn't care what he said. She was staying and going through the trunk until she found the rest of the adoption paper.

"Aim the flashlight at the stairs."

"I'm not going down," she said stubbornly.

"Sure we are."

She planned to do battle. This was too important to her. She was going to do everything she could to get answers tonight. "I need to do this."

He didn't ask why. In the dimly lit attic, he slowly

shoved the trunk across the plank floor toward the ladder.

Though grateful for his help, a more immediate problem crossed her mind. "You won't fall carrying it down, will you?"

He snorted as if the idea was ludicrous. "I don't plan to," he said in a dry tone.

She wasn't questioning his strength. Easily he, anyone, could lose balance. Despite his macho response, she raised a hand toward a corner of the trunk. "Let me help carry it?"

His don't-touch look more than his words made her yank back her hand. He descended several rungs until his right shoulder was lined up with the trunk. "Just aim the light on the ladder." He hefted the trunk onto his shoulder and, balancing it, went down the rest of the rungs.

Rachel kept the light directed at him until he reached the last one, then she hurriedly followed. He'd already entered her room.

"Here?" He eased the trunk to the floor at the foot of the bed.

"Yes, thank you." She was talking to his back. She was thankful he'd left without needing more of an explanation. She didn't want to talk. She wanted to search the trunk, learn the truth.

Even before he stepped into the hallway, she raised the lid. Thinking the paper might be caught in the folds of material, she went through everything: the worn baby blanket, Sean's baseball cap, the fuchsia-colored boa wrap. Beneath the photograph of her grandparents she found a pair of baby shoes, a silver spoon with a curved handle, lacy tablecloths, a Navy uniform, a seashell she'd given her mother, a flattened and misshapen red hat with an ostrich feather stuck in its brim. She even found her sister's doll with the messed yellow hair and gingham dress.

For a moment Rachel held the seashell to her ear. She'd given it to her mother as a welcome-home present after she'd been gone for so long.

"Rachel?"

She sat back on her heels as he came in with a coffee cup in his hand. "Is that for me?"

"I thought you might be here all night. Did you find something?"

Deliberately she tried to calm herself. She felt almost frantic to locate the rest of that letter, but she had to remain logical, not let emotion lead her. There was an explanation for all of this. There had to be. Her parents wouldn't let them live a lie. "I gave this to my mother," she said about the seashell. "I used to collect all kinds of them."

"Want this or not?" he asked about the coffee.

She stared at the cup he was holding out to her. "Yes." Setting the seashell on top of the doll first, she reached for the white mug, felt the heat on her fingertips. "That's the second time you've done something nice."

"Nice?" He was watching her closely. Had she acted too emotional earlier?

"It's not against the law to be nice," Rachel teased as an assurance to him that she was all right.

"Maybe you're easy to please."

She refused to apologize for that. "Yes, I guess I am."

"All this because I got you coffee? When was the other time?"

"You didn't have to carry down the trunk."

"You are easy to please." He gestured toward the open trunk. "Tell me now what this is about." He looked prepared to spend the night until he learned what was happening.

She held out the folded letter. "I found this tucked in one of my mother's journals." Though he took it, Rachel didn't wait for him to unfold the paper. She went on with her explanation, "It's a letter to my parents from an adoption agency. The letter states that the agency is pleased the final arrangements are almost completed for the adoption."

His dark brows bunched. "What adoption?"

"Exactly," she said, unable to mask her anger over what she was beginning to view as deceit. "What adoption?" She tightened her lips, annoyed with the tears close to breaking free. It would be dumb to get too emotional about this. She needed facts. Without them she was jumping to what might be the wrong conclusions. "I need to get answers."

"How are you going to do that?"

She hadn't gotten that far. Shock still controlled her. "I need to know if this is about my sister or myself." Before he asked, she explained why she didn't think it was about Sean. "A date would help." She pointed at her mother's other journals on the bed. "I need to read those."

He came near, squatted before her. "Rachel?" As

he caught her chin, raised her face to him, she felt him delving inside her, searching to see beyond what was visible.

She couldn't curb the feelings choking her as one question plagued her. "How could this happen and none of us know about it?" Determined to keep a tight rein on an urge to cry, she was relieved he didn't draw her into his arms, tell her there might be a mistake, offer her sympathy and comfort.

In a slow move he stood. "Take care of this. I'll watch over Heather."

"Thank you." Her mind too full of questions, she would be less attentive to Heather than she'd like to be. Bending over the trunk again, she hoped that during the repacking she might find something she'd overlooked earlier. She returned half of the mess scattered on the floor to the trunk and sat back on her heels. She needed to calm down.

Wondering where Kane was, she stood to find him. The sound of sirens filling the quiet night air drew her to the window instead. They were close. Too close.

Across the street smoke bellowed from the windows of a neighbor's house. Someone had stretched his garden hose but it ineffectually sprayed at the house. More sirens wailed to deafening loudness as fire engines whipped onto the street.

Rachel whirled away from the window. By the time she reached the front porch, a crowd had gathered on the sidewalk in front of the house.

Libby Cosley was one of the people. "Edith Bensen is in there," she said in a panic, tears filling her voice. "Someone needs to do something. Dorothy isn't home."

"Someone ran in," said a young boy standing in front of them.

"Riley." A thin man with glasses announced this to anyone who was listening.

Her heart pounding wildly, Rachel moved closer. Squinting against the smoke smarting her eyes, she fixed a stare on the steps and the porch enveloped in a fog of smoke.

"Back up, lady."

She knew someone had said something, but she couldn't take her eyes off the hazy view of the door. Time ticked by slowly. The crackling of the fire filled the night air. She sensed movement, voices around her, but she couldn't focus on anything but that doorway. Fear rose while she said a prayer. Heather didn't deserve to lose anyone else. He had to be all right. Oh, please, Lord, don't let him be hurt. Please keep him—

"Look, there!" someone yelled.

Oh, God, please. She swallowed hard against the urge to cry, elbowed her way closer. And saw him.

A shadow at first, movement in the fog of smoke, then a silhouette of a man through the haze. Above him smoke funneled into the air. The roar of the blaze competed with the shrill of more sirens.

Through the cloud, Kane appeared, carrying Mrs. Bensen in his arms. Gasping, he stumbled from the porch, down the stairs. Rachel heard shouts, those of the firemen, of bystanders. All that mattered was him.

Coughing, he laid Mrs. Bensen down on the grass.

Someone shoved an oxygen mask at him. He grabbed it, gulped air, then gave it back.

"She's breathing," one of the fireman said while slipping a mask on the elderly woman's face. Her white hair was disheveled, her face was marred with soot. But she was breathing and not harmed. Because of him.

Rachel flew at him. Not caring who saw, she flung her arms around his neck and held him. "I was so worried."

"Rachel. God," he whispered against her ear.

"Hey, you okay?" someone called out to him.

Despite the mantle of night, when he drew back from her, she saw the look of surprise on his face. "Yeah."

She heard whispers, looked around her, saw people staring. Were they finally seeing what was so obvious? she wondered. This wasn't the kind of man who'd ever walk by, let anyone down who needed his help. Were they wondering if they'd misjudged him before this, if there was a reason why he hadn't been with Charlie on that stormy night?

A fireman came near. "We need to check your vitals."

Kane predictably protested. "I'm all right."

"We still have to do this. Regulation. For our report, we have to have them."

Rachel made herself let go of him. Briefly his eyes locked with hers. She read questions in them. What she'd felt for him wouldn't simply go away because they both wanted that to happen. While a fireman cornered him, she hurried back to Heather in the house.

As she'd expected she'd slept through the excitement outside.

Rachel passed by a window. Hoses were being re-rolled. One engine had pulled away, and only a few onlookers remained. She heard the front door open and close and wandered into the living room. His back to her, he lingered near one of the windows.

She couldn't stop herself. She wanted to feel the heat of his body beneath her hands. All the fear she'd known when he'd been in that burning building was only a breath away. "You didn't get hurt, did you?" With the shake of his head, she inched close behind. Needing to touch him, she snaked her arms around his hard, flat stomach and pressed her cheek against his back. For a long moment she simply held him and reassured herself that he really was okay. "I was so afraid for you." She clung, not caring what he wanted. She needed to hold him.

She heard his sigh before he slowly turned around to face her. "Rachel." A softness threaded his voice, a softness that made her wrap her arms around his neck, tighten her embrace.

"Don't. I'll hurt you. You've been hurt enough."

"You told me that before." There had been a time when she hadn't thought she would survive all of the losses in her life. No, she didn't want to be hurt again. But all that certainty that she could ignore feelings for him had been a waste of time. She wanted to keep holding him, feel him safe in her arms. With her fingertips she brushed at the soot smudging his cheek. "Don't push me away." She wouldn't expect too much. She couldn't.

Kane felt her tremble. For him. This was wrong. He wasn't supposed to be holding her. He wasn't supposed to want the feel of her soft curves against him. But even the scent of her so near made him feel more alive. All he could think about was filling himself with her taste, with the softness, the sweetness of her lips. All he wanted to do was kiss her until they were both gasping for breath.

He lowered his hand, let it drift down her back to the curve of her waist. He'd washed his hands when he'd come in, but his clothes held the smell of smoke, carried soot on them. "I'll get you dirty," he murmured against her neck.

"It doesn't matter."

His face inches from hers, he searched her eyes. Here was the real problem. She was so sweet, so warm, so willing. And nothing mattered but her.

Framing her face with his hands, he closed his mouth over hers. She'd stunned him earlier. She wasn't supposed to care so much about him. When she'd rushed to him without a care about the people around them and had fallen into his arms, an ache had begun, an ache he could only appease if he held her like this. Now with her scent intoxicating him, he couldn't pull back. He didn't want to think, only feel. Hunger took over as he felt a willingness in the lips clinging to his.

He'd known she would feel this way in his arms. As desire curled around him, he captured her breaths in his mouth. Even as he knew he should pull away, he gathered her in his arms. "Be sure," he murmured against her hair before he lowered her to the bed.

She refused to let him draw away. With one hand tight against his back, her other hand sought his waist, yanked at the snap on his jeans. She turned her face up to him, her lips parting in invitation. "I'm sure."

Stupidly he'd thought he could walk away if she'd said no, but the moment her lips warmed his, all the willpower to stop dissolved. He stretched out beside her. He'd have thought he was dreaming if she hadn't touched him then.

As she inched her hands up under his shirt, her fingers fluttering across his flesh, his skin felt on fire. For a second—only a second—sensations held him still. Then he hooked a finger at the hem of her scooped T-shirt, lowered his head and kissed the silky skin that was exposed above the waistband of her jeans. He could have moved on. Instead he licked it, traced her navel with his tongue. On a low moan, she undulated her hips. And drove him crazy.

Slowly he raised the shirt, tasted more of her flesh until he reached the lacy edge of her bra. Soft hands moved more frantically over his back, beckoned him. He unclasped the bra's front clip, lowered his mouth to the round softness, to the erect nipple. "You're beautiful. You always were," he whispered, revealing the fascination for her that he'd struggled against.

A fantasy he'd never expected to experience was his for the taking. From low in his throat he moaned when her hand wedged between them. She called out his name on a long breath while her fingers found his zipper. From day one, he'd wanted to be with her like this. Sixteen years ago he'd longed for her. Now—now desire clawed at him.

Drowning in her taste, he groped to pull down her jeans, to roll the wispy silk of her panties over her hips, to find the heat and softness of her. He thought he had control. But she did. Gently her fingers dipped inside his briefs and closed over him. Her stroke nearly undid him.

At first tentatively, then more boldly she touched him. Weakened him, pleasured him. Nothing prepared him for her giving, for her willingness to please. She was sweet and soft and tender. And she wanted him.

That one thought returned over and over as he scooted down, skimmed a hand along the curve of her waist. With a gentleness he hadn't known he possessed, he sought the heat between her thighs. They parted, welcomed him. Slowly he caressed velvety flesh, stroked it, lowered his mouth to taste it.

A low sigh as if it came from deep in her chest floated over him. "Kane." His name whispered on the air. She was his. At that moment every fantasy he'd ever had about her came true.

He felt a weakness flood him. A desperation stirred to bury himself in her, to feel the heat rise between them. With a simple touch, she snatched breath from him. Throbbing now, he waited only for her shudder. He wouldn't have lasted longer. Couldn't wait. Fumbling, he found the foil package in the drawer of the bedside table. Then he poised above her.

In the moonlit room, her eyes were hooded with passion. A smile touched her lips as he entered her, gently at first, and then again harder. Eyes closing, she moaned his name. That it was him she wanted was all that mattered. When her legs embraced his hips, tightened him to her, he was already lost in her. He shut his eyes, let her heat envelop him and gave in to the frenzy between them.

There was an instant when he thought his heart might never beat normally again. With her still in his arms, he grabbed a long, unsteady breath and rolled to his back. "You should have stopped me." He wanted to tell her that she'd been wonderful, that she'd surpassed every fantasy he'd had about her. He wanted to tell her that he was aching to be with her again. But he didn't say any of that. "I'm trouble for you."

Despite his words, she tilted her face up to him and smiled. "There you go—boasting again."

He never expected her to respond with a tease. He was being serious, trying to warn her, and she wasn't listening.

She laughed against the curve of his neck. "Are you serious? I wanted you," she said in a voice so soft it slithered a sensation through him like a seduction.

"That was then. What about now?" Lightly he caressed the curve of her bare hip. "I'm not going to give you what you want, Rachel."

"I don't expect anything but this," she said softly.

He'd wanted her to tell him that, but deep down he felt a pang of disappointment. He was honest enough with himself to know he still wished for more. It didn't matter that he had no business wishing for anything with her.

"We could do that again," she whispered.

Closing his eyes, he buried his face in her hair. She could make him wish. She could make him yearn for more, a lot more. "Rachel—"

"In a little while—when you're ready."

She'd misunderstood his hesitation. With her mouth near his and her fingers enticing him, desire came on a rush. "I'm almost…ready."

She laughed as he pressed himself against her thigh. "Yes, you are."

Hours later the faint hint of dawn bathed the room in a gray light. Though the scent and heat of her lingered in the bed, she'd left minutes ago. For several seconds he stared up at the ceiling, pretended he still heard her soft breathing beside him as it had been through the night.

There was danger in that kind of thinking. He shouldn't want this to be anything but an enjoyable, satisfying time with a beautiful woman, but still he wished he'd awakened with her next to him.

Barely moving, he angled a look to the side to see the alarm clock. Five-fifteen. At six-thirty he was scheduled to meet a group of men, college buddies who were out for a day of fishing. He roused himself from the bed and headed for the shower.

He'd never brought a woman to the house, to his bed before. He went to their homes where he controlled the moment when the evening ended, where he could leave before the time together became more than an enjoyable romp in bed by consenting adults.

For a moment he let the water beat at him. This would be different. He'd find her in the kitchen. Already he smelled the coffee brewing. She'd be dressed in that yellow, sensible-looking, tailored robe that tied at the waist, flowed to her ankles and showed nothing. He didn't need to see. He knew the taste and feel of the flesh beneath the cloth, hungered just thinking about it.

He stepped out of the shower and snatched a towel from the wall rod. For her sake he shouldn't get more involved with her. *You are involved. She's living in your home. She's taking care of a child who's of your blood. She's slept in your bed. You buried yourself in her.* What now? He had no answer. He simply wanted to see her, and hold her again.

Minutes later, unobserved, he lounged in the kitchen doorway and watched her. Seated on a kitchen chair, her hair mussed from sleep and from his fingers, she held Heather in her arms. In a soft musical tone she cooed to her while she fed her the bottle. Too homey. Too much like a family. And too close to perfect.

As if sensing he was near, slowly she raised her head. "Good morning." A smile spread from her lips to her eyes, incredible green eyes that were filled with delight—for him.

"Have you been up long?"

"We were hungry early," she said lightly. She

lifted Heather to her shoulder and patted her back. "Do you have time for breakfast?"

He almost said no. Almost. He knew if he refused, if he rushed out, he'd hurt her. It was a way to break this off quickly, before they went any deeper. But he couldn't do it. He couldn't willingly be responsible for taking the sparkle out of her eyes. "I'll cook."

The smile spread to her lips. "Do you have a specialty?"

Keep it light. If he kept things airy and lighthearted between them this morning, she might not get serious about everything. It didn't matter what she'd said last night about not expecting more. Rachel was all heart, felt too much. "Cereal," he finally answered.

A laugh slipped into her voice. With Heather's burp, Rachel bent over, lowered her to the infant seat. "Bet you pour a great bowl."

"You have two choices." He flung open a cabinet door. "Corn flakes or—"

She moved near, behind him, so close her breath fanned the side of his neck. "Or what?" she asked, gently nibbling on his ear.

Weak. She made him so weak that he nearly shut his eyes. Facing her, he gave in to a fascination to touch a strand of hair by her cheek. The instant his fingers made contact with her flesh, she angled her face toward his hand. Softly she pressed her lips to his palm—and nearly unmanned him. The gesture was so sweet, so accepting, so tender. Had anyone ever touched him like that?

"And what?" she murmured.

Oh, God. Enough of this. It didn't matter if her feelings got hurt. Better to cause that now, than to lead her along, hurt her later when she'd invested too much emotion in them. "Whatever else is in the cabinet," he said, taking an abrupt step back from her.

Behind him he heard her sigh. He'd thought the act would force her to face their relationship honestly. As he'd just done, he would hurt her even more if this went on.

"It bothers you when you let emotion go, doesn't it?" she challenged instead of accepting the rebuff.

Kane shot a hard look at her. It occurred to him just how much he'd miscalculated her response. He couldn't—didn't dare—give anything back—ever. When would she realize that?

"You're not annoyed with me. You're upset with yourself because you feel something for me, because it was good last night."

Too good, he could have told her. By the stubborn tilt of her head, she wasn't ready to accept what he was trying to make her understand.

"What is it you really want to say? Do you regret this?"

"Not for myself." He wanted her to know that.

"Oh, Kane. For me?" Softness came into her eyes, her voice. "I don't need protection. I'm thirty-one years old. I know what I want. I know when I want to be with a man. I wanted to be with you. I'm not going to regret that."

Damn. Why didn't she give up? "You have no regrets?"

''Not one.'' True, Rachel admitted to herself, she hadn't considered the consequences of last night. She'd kissed and tasted, she'd let the force of desire bind her to him. She'd thought she'd go mad with hunger, and even after having him, she'd wanted more.

''Rachel, we're complicating everything.''

''Probably,'' she answered, meeting his stare with a steady one of her own. She'd sensed that he wanted to make himself resent what had happened between them. She didn't take personally what another woman might view as rejection. She believed he would push anyone away who got too close.

More than once he'd made it clear that he worried about hurting her. He had some misguided notion that he needed to protect people from him. She assured herself that she wouldn't be hurt if she didn't let herself get carried away with what was happening between them. Somehow she'd keep her feet firmly planted on the ground. She wasn't stupid. She'd show caution. But she wouldn't agree to diminishing how wonderful it had been. ''We can do this.''

Troubled eyes met hers. With all the gentleness she'd known the night before, he framed her face with his hands. She'd felt those same, strong, callused hands, those tender hands, stroking and caressing every inch of her last night. ''Rachel, just remember it won't—''

She raised a hand, silenced him with her fingertips. He didn't need to speak. In his eyes she read a message. *It won't last.* She could have told him that she didn't need any guarantees. She'd learned they didn't exist. Self-preservation insisted that she not expect any. She was no more interested in a commitment than he was. No matter how many nights they spent together, she wouldn't let herself become caught up with his tenderness, or the sense of belonging she felt with him and Heather. And she wouldn't fall in love with them.

Chapter Ten

Certain he'd need to leave soon, Rachel crossed to the cupboard for cereal bowls while he answered a phone call.

From Kane's side of the conversation, she gathered he was talking to Lonnie. He confirmed that, after returning the receiver to its hook on the wall. "Something's wrong with a swivel mechanism on one of the fighting chairs." In between a few spoons of the doughnut-shaped cereal, he mentioned overhauling the engine of the *Sea Siren* before the Fourth of July weekend. "We're booked solid for the night cruise."

Once she'd gone with her family on a boat, and from the ocean they'd watched the fireworks display. It had been spectacular, colors exploding in the sky, reflecting on the dark water.

"Where will you watch the fireworks?"

''I'm not sure yet.'' She went to the sink to rinse out Heather's bottle. She couldn't help wondering if he was looking for a logical excuse to stay at the boat and avoid the house.

Behind her, she heard him punching out a phone number, then asking for Lou Banning. What thought had sparked that action? she wondered. Was he thinking about the upcoming holiday, that if he didn't begin the process to find Heather's father, then they'd both still be with him by the next holiday? Mentally she shook her head. Quit trying to do the impossible—mind read—she berated herself, and listened to him give the private investigator the names of the three men Marnie had dated.

''Yeah, probably a DNA would confirm it,'' he said in response to something the man said before finishing the call.

Rachel propped Heather's washed bottle on the drainboard and faced him. ''Heather has a doctor's appointment.''

Bent over the counter, he jotted a note on a small pad of paper. ''Routine?''

''The doctor requested a follow-up about her cold because of how easily ear infections hit little ones.'' Rachel dried her hands on a kitchen towel. Would he leave as he had every other morning, or this morning would he kiss her goodbye? She'd like that. Just because she needed to be sensible about their relationship didn't mean she couldn't enjoy being with him now. And as much as she had claimed to him that nothing had changed, everything was different this morning. "Did the private investigator say how long it would take?"

He slipped the paper into the small front pocket of his jeans. "With all the information you gave me about them, he didn't think it would take long."

And then Heather would be gone from her life. *You can't have either of them, Rachel.* Silently she said it several times like a mantra, fought the melancholy that was a breath away from grabbing hold. She didn't want to love another man and a baby, believe they were in her life and one day find them gone from it.

Caught up in thoughts, she jerked, startled to find his hand at her face. Tenderly he grazed his knuckles across her cheek. "Rachel, what am I going to do with you?"

It wasn't a question. It was a plea for help to stop this before more happened. "Kiss me," she whispered, and coiled her arms around his neck.

Within an hour she was pushing Heather's carriage into the doctor's office. While she was in the waiting room, Rachel's thoughts returned to the search she had ahead of her to learn about the adoption. Somehow she'd get answers, she thought determinedly.

"You had quite a bit of excitement last evening." LeeAnn was off, and the doctor's other nurse, an ample-figured, gray-haired woman led Rachel toward a room. Barbara Tibbs delivered a dimpled smile at Rachel. "I heard we have a hero in town," she went on now. "Glad folks are finally realizing what I've known all along."

Trying not to seem too interested in what the

woman was saying about Kane, Rachel lowered Heather onto the examination table. "What's that?" she asked while she slipped Heather's legs out of her pink-and-white sleeper.

"That Kane Riley's too fine a man to do what they'd believed."

Rachel paused, thrilled to find someone else who believed in him. "Do you know him well?"

"I knew Charlie well enough. Charlie raved about him, and he wasn't easily fooled."

"Do you know what happened the night Charlie died?" Rachel asked louder as Heather began complaining about being undressed.

"No, I don't," Barbara said. "But Charlie believed in him. That's enough for me," she added. Rachel wished she'd had time to say more, but Barbara stepped aside as the pediatrician ambled in.

He smiled at Rachel then, and again when he finished his examination of Heather's ears. She was doing better, he said. While that's what Rachel had hoped he'd say, and was pleased, Heather wailed her displeasure about everything from being undressed to being redressed and didn't stop until she was snug in her carriage again.

Nothing was simple anymore, Kane decided. He'd honestly never expected any of this to happen with her. Oh, sure, he'd fantasized about it. Sixteen years ago he'd fallen asleep thinking about a long, sweet night with her. But he was no longer that boy. He'd known that a person didn't get everything they wanted.

Yet he had last night. And an unexpected wave of contentment swept through him. He didn't want to think beyond it, dissect reasons for it. But for the first time since he'd started working on a boat, he wanted to be somewhere else.

"Everyone's aboard," Lonnie said, cutting into his thoughts as he boarded the boat. "You sure keep things tight to your chest." He gave Kane a Cheshire Cat grin. "Someone said that you have your sister's baby."

Kane would guess that Velma Monroe was that someone. "What else?"

"That your sister died. I'm sorry. That must have been rough."

No one would know how bad. The only thing he and Marnie had had for so long was each other. Since her death there were mornings that he awakened still filled with disbelief that she wasn't near anymore. "Unexpected," he told Lonnie.

"I never thought of you as the daddy type." Lonnie laughed when he'd said those words, as if they were ridiculous.

How wrong he was. Kane had always wanted that most of all. As kids, Marnie had longed for the clothes others could afford and she couldn't. He'd yearned for what had been lost. He remembered a time before his mother had died. He remembered laughter, his parents hugging. He remembered when they'd been a family, before his world had shattered.

Aboard the boat he made contact with the men who'd hired it, then motored them out to sea. Overhead seagulls circled. Bantering and laughing, the men on the boat lounged in the fighting chairs. The wind held a coolness, though it was the middle of summer. He licked his bottom lip, tasted the salty breeze, but Rachel's sweeter taste came to mind.

She'd kissed him long and hard before he'd left the house. She weakened him. She'd made him vulnerable with her tender heart when she'd said she was worried about him last night. All of this had happened because he'd been vulnerable then.

Yeah, sounds good. But he had no excuse this morning. When she'd wrapped her arms around him again, he'd forgotten everything except how wonderful it felt to hold her. And she made him want what he'd vowed never to look for. *Love.*

Decadent. Rachel could think of no other word to describe the chocolate-fudge cake with the scoop of French vanilla ice cream, a dollop of whipped cream and a cherry. She watched a woman at another table consuming it, savoring each mouthful. Benny's Café hadn't disappointed her. It still sold her favorite dessert.

Through the wall of windows in the café, she saw Lori and waved.

Smiling broadly, Lori breezed into the café and toward her. "I should have known I'd find you here. Are you eyeing the fudge cake?"

"I'm having a hard time resisting," Rachel admitted. "I took Heather to the doctor's office, ran some errands, then stopped at the library. But after about an hour, a craving for the cake began."

Lori laughed. "You always were weak to it."

"Always."

Smiling, Lori bent over Heather's carriage and gently stroked her soft, dark hair. "She is so adorable. So beautiful. All Rileys are good looking. I remember my mother saying that Kane's father had been the handsomest man in town before he started drinking." She shrugged one shoulder. "He's the topic of conversation this morning. Kane, not his father. People are saying he's a hero."

That brought Rachel's head up. "They are?" She felt something warm spread through her. "They really are?"

Lori slid into the booth seat across from her. "Did he really run into the house and rescue Mrs. Bensen?"

"Yes, he really did." She didn't hesitate to toot a horn on his behalf. "But he would. He'd never turn his back on someone who needed help."

Hunching toward her, Lori gave her a sly smile. "You'd stick by him no matter what anyone else said, wouldn't you?"

Because she'd seen a side of him that he kept hidden from others. She knew his tenderness, his compassion, had seen his torment, too, and his guilt. But that was his business. No one else's. "I know he isn't like what people say."

An inquisitive quality slipped into Lori's voice. "You learned what happened with Charlie Greer, then? Why Kane was in Bangor instead of here with him?"

"No, but it doesn't matter." She acknowledged that she'd developed blind faith in him, would defend

him to the hilt. "I'm sure he had a good reason."
Silence seemed best at the moment. Looking away
from her friend's distressed expression, she watched
the lady next to her jam another forkful of cake in
her mouth. Lori had been the second person today to
mention Kane with praise. She hoped, really hoped,
for Kane's sake, that people were realizing they might
have misjudged him.

Before leaving, Lori promised to phone and finalize
plans to meet for the Fourth of July parade. Alone,
Rachel resumed reading until a waitress came by.

While pouring coffee, the woman gushed over
Heather. "She's a real pretty baby. I—" She quieted,
her eyes on the door and the café's newest customer.

No silverware clinked, no voices murmured in private conversation as Kane entered. He scanned the
café, then his eyes locked with hers.

He was a foot away when she noticed the seashell
in his hand. The size of his palm, horn shaped, pink-
ish and pearly looking, it was absolutely beautiful. He
set it on the table in front of her while taking the seat
Lori had vacated.

Pleasure swept through her. She'd been romanced,
given flowers and candy, and wined and dined, but
she'd never felt a smidgen of excitement like this before. The gift was unimportant. What it meant mattered more. He'd been thinking about her while he
was gone. He'd wanted to please her. "I love it."
She felt eyes on them, didn't care. "I wish we were
alone."

A questioning look washed over his face. "Why?"

Her spirits high, she laughed. "So I could kiss you, of course."

"Rachel?"

She laughed again. Around them conversation stopped. Heads swung in their direction. "I love it when you get that tone like only you know what's best."

He released a snort, but a smile in his eyes belied his grumbling. "Glad I'm amusing you."

She couldn't help it. She giggled. Leaning forward, she slipped a hand over his strong, callused one. "Why aren't you on the boat?"

"I wanted to get something at the discount store." He craned his neck to see Heather. "What did the doctor say about her?"

Rachel followed his shift in conversation. "She's fine." With Heather's squeaking, she bent toward her. "You're such a good girl," she soothed. She was a perfect baby. Except for the bout with the stuffy nose, she usually only cried when hungry. "Do you have to go back to the boat now? If not, we could go. I'll make you something to eat for lunch."

A smile nudged up the corners of his mouth. "Hungry?"

She let another laugh ripple out. "Guess I am." He'd mentioned a late-afternoon cruise. She doubted he'd have time for more than lunch, but the teasing talk was fun.

"I'll pay the bill."

Rachel smiled after him, delighted to have the unexpected afternoon with him. Maneuvering Heather's carriage around tables, she nodded a greeting to two women in a nearby booth whose eyes had fixed on her and Kane. "Ready?" she asked when she joined Kane at the register near the door.

"Almost." He was waiting for change when Benny, the café's owner, a stoop-shouldered, white-haired man in his midsixties, came from his office. "Afternoon, Rachel. Riley." The greeting was said with some reluctance to Kane, but yesterday morning he would have been ignored. That people were acknowledging him and saying hello was progress. "I thought you would want to know. Mrs. Bensen is doing okay."

"He already knows," a feminine voice behind them cut in.

Rachel swung around to see Dorothy Bensen, the woman's daughter. "One of the nurses at the hospital, the one who went to school with you, Kane, recognized your voice when you called early this morning to ask about my mother. Thank you."

Kane reacted with a nod of the head, nothing more, but Rachel noted a softening in his features. "You're surprised," she said when they were outside.

"I'm not used to anyone, except Lonnie and strangers, saying so much to me."

Rachel followed the command of his hand under her elbow to cross the street. "If you'd tell them what really happened that night, they wouldn't act the way they do."

Annoyance dashed into his eyes. "How do you know what they're thinking isn't what really happened?"

She refused to let him weaken her belief in him.

"Because I've been held by you." Only feet from her van, Rachel halted, forcing him to stop. "Because I believe in you."

She watched him visibly draw in a breath, could tell he was touched by her words. In a gesture of resignation, he lowered his forehead to hers. "Is there any point in arguing with you?"

Just being this close to him made her yearn. "None."

They arrived home within seconds of each other. While he was unloading a huge carton from the bed of his truck, Rachel carried Heather in and changed her diaper. When she reentered the kitchen, she saw him yanking at the sides of the long, rectangular-shaped carton. "What is…? Oh!" She smiled as he slowly unpacked a play yard for Heather from the blue denim tote bag. Made of matching blue fabric, the play yard had cartoon characters printed on the base.

"I thought she could use this. Where do you want it? Here?"

Rachel abandoned her study of the bright-yellow Tweety bird. "Yes." Hope threaded through her that he was allowing himself to care. Little by little, he must be opening his heart to his niece. "Why did you buy it?"

Head bent, he unfolded the sides. "She needs kicking room. It'll be good for her."

Rachel didn't dare say more, sensing if she offered words about how nice that he'd bought it, he'd resist and back up two steps again. Of course, that irascible and often difficult side of him was almost becoming endearing to her. "Let's see how she likes it."

All the while they were eating ham and cheese omelets, Heather expressed her joy by gurgling and kicking her legs. He made both of us happy today, Rachel reflected, remembering her own delight when he'd handed her the seashell. She thought he'd looked pleased before he'd returned outside to his truck to unload driftwood that he sold to one of the souvenir shops.

Done with the dishes, she used the time to herself to search through the journals for answers. She'd read only one passage when the opening of the door made her look up.

Kane dropped a stack of paperwork on the counter before coming near the sink to wash his hands. "Are you getting ready to leave?"

He leveled a quizzical look at her. "Do you want me to leave?"

On a laugh, she went to him and leaned close to spread light kisses along the strong column of his neck. "Trying to get me to say that I wish you were staying?"

A low chuckle answered her. Grinning, he took her face in his damp hands. "Guess you just did." With a more serious look, he stared past her. Rachel traced his stare to the diary. "Did you learn more?" he asked.

"A little." He released her, and showing curiosity, he went to the table. Rachel joined him, and over his shoulder, read her mother's words.

A woman from the adoption agency came today. This was her second visit. I don't know why we need to go through all this. I'm feeling angry, and I know that isn't good. But this all seems such a waste of time. The mother is willing to let the baby go when it's born, and I'm willing to take it, so why all of these visits?

Because of me, I suppose. I have a history of a mental disorder. No one understands. I'm fine now. I simply couldn't cope for a while with my loss. I hope none of this hurts our chances. I want the baby.

Alan asked again if I was sure that I did. To refuse is unthinkable. How could I not want it? What I can't understand is how the woman can give it up. Oh, what do I care? To have a baby again in my arms is to have prayers answered.

Kane raised his gaze to her. "Isn't it unusual for the adoptive parents to know the biological mother?"

"I don't know." She was still wondering how her mother could bring another child into her life, chance having another piece of her heart sliced away. "I keep wondering why they would want to adopt if they already had children."

He faced her, but was silent—too long. Why he wasn't saying anything seemed fairly obvious.

"You're thinking they might not have had any then?" she asked, then shook her head. "No, you're wrong."

"Is that denial?"

She hadn't realized how much she'd begun to depend on him until that moment. He'd become one of a few people she trusted enough to share her thoughts with, who knew this family secret. "No, it isn't. My mother mentions wanting the baby, hoping her illness won't hurt their chances to adopt it. Sean and I were around when she got ill."

"So what does that mean? The baby was your sister?"

Everything was so confusing. "That seems to be the only logical answer. But—"

"But what?"

"She looks like us. At least, I always thought she did. She has red hair, green eyes."

"Couldn't your parents have looked for a child who'd resemble you and your brother?"

"I suppose so." At the hint of anger in her voice, she labored for a calming breath. "You know what I can't understand," she said, quieter. "They lied to us, Kane. They never told us the truth, never mentioned that one of us was adopted. They should have. It's not fair to let someone go their whole life and not know where they really came from. If it had been me, I would have wanted to know the name of my real parents, where they live, why they let me go." She let him hear her confusion. "How could the people who claim to love you tell such a lie?"

He fingered strands of her hair. "You could be jumping to the wrong conclusion."

Oh, she prayed she was. "You're right. I'm being unfair." She didn't have all the facts. Wasn't this what people in town had done to him? She should find out when plans to adopt had begun, she thought, while thumbing through pages.

"I'll be right back."

Rachel nodded in response, but Kane could have been giving her a weather report. The words in the journal held her spellbound.

February 20
Another woman is having his child. Another woman, not me.

Rachel kept staring at the words. She'd misread. She was sure of it. Slowly she reread them, then turned a page, read, turned another. Almost frantically she kept turning them, looking for something to tell her she'd gotten the wrong idea from her mother's words. Her mother had been ill. When she'd lost touch with reality she might have believed that he'd done such a thing when he hadn't.

When had she been ill? Rachel flipped pages to find that short passage about being tired. It was on September 2 of the previous year.

She skimmed more pages. Confirmation of what she'd begun to believe came in her mother's own handwriting on the following January.

January 6
Alan had been so despondent at Christmas time. I know he tried hard to keep Christmas normal for Rachel and Sean. It couldn't have been easy with me in the hospital. I remember so little of that now, but they tell me I was incoherent. Poor

Alan. I understand his need to be held, comforted. He's so full of self-recrimination, of guilt about the affair.

Affair. An affair? The words were right in front of her in her mother's handwriting. She hadn't been in the hospital when she'd wrote it. On January 6, she'd been writing about a time that had passed, a time when her husband had been alone, when he'd broken his marriage vows.

January 26
Alan thinks I can't forgive him. I thought I might not be able to, but I'm able to look back and remember what happened. I only wish now that he hadn't had to grieve alone for the sweet baby we lost, but I couldn't help him. So many months passed in the hospital before I stopped living in denial after I miscarried. If only I'd been stronger. If only I'd been the one Alan could have reached for. Instead another woman had given him comfort.

Her throat suddenly dry, Rachel moved to the sink. Breathing hard, she curled her fingers around the edge of the counter for a long moment before she grabbed a glass. She gulped down water, her mind racing.

"Rachel, why are you crying?"

She snapped her back straight. With a fingertip, she rubbed at her cheek, at tears she hadn't even been aware of. Pivoting away, she fussed with a kitchen towel, making much about the folds. When Kane brought his arm across her chest, drew her back against him, she shook her head, still trying to deny what she'd read seconds ago.

"He was with someone else," she managed to say. The words caught in her throat. "He—my father was unfaithful to her." She felt such humiliation, such fury, so much grief, as if she'd lost him seconds ago instead of years before. Needing space around her, she pulled free of Kane's embrace to say wrenching words. "The baby was his and—another woman's."

Ignoring her effort to step away, he held her tightly to him again, pressed his face to hers.

Rachel closed her eyes. "How could he?"

He held firm as if aware how much she wanted to go somewhere, be alone, curl up and forget.

"How could he?" she murmured again, and choked back tears.

Chapter Eleven

Oh, God, how would she tell her sister? Rachel made herself draw back. "I don't know how to handle this. How do I tell my sister that her mother was some unknown woman our father had an affair with?" In the past she'd weathered some difficult times and had coped. Of course, the image of someone dear, of a man she'd believed could do no wrong, had never been shattered before. It was as if her father had died all over again.

"Do you have to do this alone?"

She gave him a weak smile for the reminder. "No. No, I guess I don't." Her brother and sister were adults now. Whatever truth she uncovered needed to be faced by all of them.

"What kind of person is your sister?"

"Cheerful, optimistic, adventurous." And she'd

have a hard time with this. While Rachel had been closer to her father, as the baby, the youngest, Gillian had not only trailed their mother everywhere, but she'd also been daddy's little girl. "She'll hide her hurt." Her shock. Gillian would be stunned. Who wouldn't be to learn about being adopted, to learn the mother you loved wasn't the one who gave birth to you.

"Do what you need to."

Only then did she hear Heather's wail.

"I'll take care of her."

"Thank you." She was thankful that he wasn't the type to force sympathy. She didn't need to talk out her feelings. She didn't need soft words now. Decisions needed to be made. Hard ones. The world she'd always known, all the happy days and the memories of her youth had been spoiled by what she'd learned.

Don't get ahead of yourself, a small voice nagged. A slim possibility still existed that none of what she believed was true. A talk with her practical, logical brother would help calm her. He'd talk in terms of legalities. He'd keep emotion at bay. He was good at that, the result of too much of his own heartbreak since his divorce.

Quickly she punched out his home phone number. Wanting to sound calmer than she felt, she drew several deep breaths. But when she heard his hello, she hadn't composed herself and rushed the words. "Something has happened."

Anxiety laced his voice. "To you?"

"No," she said to abate the worry she heard in his tone. "And not Gillian, either," she said, though that

wasn't entirely true. "Sean, I found Mama's diaries."
She waited a moment. "I...I learned something."

He sort of laughed. "You're not usually so vague.
Out with it, sis."

She whipped out words, revealing everything she'd
learned.

"We need more proof."

Good. She'd hoped he'd say that. A cautious man,
he'd gauge the situation thoroughly before suggesting
action. "I don't think I should call Gillian yet." It
was a phone call she wanted to avoid as long as possible. "And last time we talked she was heading for
San Francisco for a hairstylists' convention."

"Find out more first. She doesn't need to be upset
for nothing."

She was grateful he'd reinforced her thoughts not
to stir Gillian up when they didn't have all the facts.

"Are you leaving there?" he asked, turning the
conversation toward her.

It was a question she wasn't prepared for. For a
second she stalled, but she knew him. The longer she
was quiet, the more inclined he'd be to believe she
was hiding something. And to lie to him was unthinkable. Mentally she prepared for his advice. How could
she explain to him that reasons for staying out-
weighed those for her to leave? "Not yet, Sean."

Her brother was disturbingly quiet. He was wor-
rying, she knew. But she needed to stay, not only for
Heather but also for herself. Someone in town must
know about the child, her father's child, that her
mother had agreed to adopt.

"Let me know if you learn more about the woman," he said.

"I will," she assured him before offering a good-bye.

A sound at the doorway made her look up. She realized it was the creak of a floorboard. Kane stood with Heather snuggled against his chest. "My brother agrees with me that we should learn more." She checked the wall clock and held out her arms to take Heather from him. "It's time for you to leave."

He kept the baby against him a moment longer, patted her back. "Not if you need me to stay."

She felt a deeper meaning in those words and was touched that he'd asked, that he had been willing to give her whatever support she needed. There was a time when she'd hoped for a soul mate, someone who would share her joys and sadness. She'd thought that person would be Keith. Now she knew that she had to stand alone. "No, I'll be fine."

Trusting that she was leveling with him, Kane left for the pier. He'd wanted to offer words that would ease away her anguish. He'd been willing to offer her a shoulder if she needed it, but comforting, being one of those supersensitive, modern guys was a stretch for him. He never knew what to say, what words were right when a woman was sad or crying. Hell, a woman's tears always sent sweat running down his body.

He figured he owed her, though. She'd put her life on hold to come here, to make sure Heather was where she belonged. He didn't know what he would have done without her, and wished now for some way to make everything easier for her.

Running late, he sped toward the dock. Luck accompanied him or he'd have run into Hubbard Bay's sheriff, a poker buddy of Charlie's.

Charlie Greer had touched a lot of lives, Kane's most of all. All that he had was because of Charlie. Sometimes he'd imagine the old man standing on the deck of the *Maggie Lee,* his captain's hat set low, his eyes squinting against the sun. Tanned and weathered with a white beard, he'd been a short man with a strong, sturdy build even though he'd been two months short of his seventy-fourth birthday. He'd been Kane's hero. He'd been his rescuer, his savior.

Nearing the dock, Kane noted six couples, chic Californians in their midthirties to forties, boarding the *Maggie Lee.* He parked his truck, dashed into the bait shop, then jumped on deck to join Lonnie starboard. "You got lunch for them?"

"Did." With a couple of sentences he offered Kane a rundown on their passengers.

Kane nodded at the right moments, but his thoughts were elsewhere. Stepping away, he headed to the wheelhouse while Lonnie moseyed over to play the *Maggie Lee*'s version of a cruise director.

If Kane hired someone else to man one of the boats, he could double his business. Finding someone he'd trust that much proved difficult. He'd like it to be Lonnie, but his deckhand wasn't showing much staying power.

If they were closer, Lonnie might feel more loyal, but Kane had never opened easily to people, and now, more than before, he shunned closeness. Even when he'd been a kid, he hadn't fit in, and he'd learned it was more comfortable to stay on the outside, keep to himself.

After his mother had died, the only one who'd mattered to him had been Marnie and Charlie. Charlie Greer had given him hope that he could make enough money to move Marnie and him into their own place. Then she'd split. He'd have been in limbo if Charlie hadn't given him a purpose in life. And look how he'd paid Charlie back. The captain had deserved better.

So did Rachel. She had a world of her own troubles now. He didn't need to give her more.

At the stove Rachel waited for the teakettle's whistle and cast an eye out the window at a darkening sky. Growing anxious, she switched on the radio to catch a weather report. Warnings of a northeaster made her wish Kane was home. How easily worry could rush over her.

If the weather turned more threatening, Kane would head back to port. He'd said that he cherished his boats too much to risk them. But she knew he possessed deeper values and would never do anything to harm others. That's why the blame he carried about Charlie and about his sister rang out as ridiculous to her.

So she could watch the weather, she dropped to a chair near the living room windows, then opened her mother's journal to the days after the first entry about the baby.

February 30

We're going to take the child. I'm thrilled. Boy or girl. That doesn't matter to me. I'm so glad. I'd thought Alan would refuse. He told me this morning he can't believe I didn't refuse. Oh, how to make him understand. I want his child, even this child by another woman.

It should be easy for me to adopt the baby. Step-parent adoptions are the easiest. After all, one parent is the biological one. Oh, won't it be lovely to hold a child again.

Who was the other woman? Rachel needed to know her name. The longer she kept what she'd learned from Gillian, the more guilty she felt. She raced through pages, mostly ones containing her mother's meanderings about something cute Sean had done, or how glad she was to be well now. A few entries stirred Rachel's smiles. She stopped at an early August entry.

I feel as if a piece of me is gone again. L.S. changed her mind. Why do I keep losing babies?

L.S.? Were those the woman's initials? Was she someone still living in town?

She reread the other line. ''Why do I keep losing babies.'' Sitting back, she closed her eyes. Though she felt for her mother, she said a prayer of thanks. If the baby's mother had changed her mind, then her mother had never adopted their father's child by L.S. Gillian wasn't the baby. She couldn't stop her next thought. Thank God, she learned that before calling her sister.

A crack of lightning snagged her attention. In the distance thunder roared. She reached for her cup of tea and nearly spilled it as the phone shrilled.

"Guess who?" a female voice sang in response to Rachel's hello. The caller laughed, then announced, "It's Tracy."

"Oh, Tracy." Somewhat relieved by the latest information, she brought up a smile in her voice for her friend. "How are you?"

Tracy's special infectious laugh pleased Rachel. "I would have called sooner, but we've been out of town. We have to get together for lunch. Tomorrow, okay?"

"I'd love to," Rachel assured her. As the wind rattled windows, her gaze shifted to the darkness outside. Rain began in a rush, pounding hard and furious. Concern for Kane mounted within her.

"Great. Wait," she said abruptly as if jerking herself back to the conversation. "Why don't you come to our house for the Fourth of July celebration, too, watch the fireworks with us?"

Us was her and Dean Jerick. He'd been as shy as Tracy, a studious boy with horn-rimmed glasses. They had two daughters under five. "I'll let you know tomorrow." Anxious, with the click of the door, she started for it.

"Lori told me about Marnie."

Rachel forced her attention back to Tracy, responded to her words of genuine sympathy for their loss of a friend.

"I liked her brother. Quiet." She laughed. "But then so was I. See if you can get him to come with you."

"I know he can't. He runs the *Sea Siren.*"

"Oh, that's right. He's probably working that night, huh?"

"Yes, he is," Rachel answered, and felt relief swoop through her as Kane came in. She smiled, then quickly eased out of the phone call with Tracy to greet him. The storm darkened the room. Relieved he was home, she stepped close. "Did you hit bad weather before you got in?"

He wiped a hand across his damp face. "We came in ahead of it."

It didn't matter that she wasn't supposed to care too much. She couldn't switch off feelings, pretend no concern for him. Slipping her arms around his neck, she kissed him, felt the hint of a smile beneath her lips. For a long moment she lost herself in the sweet, savoring tenderness of the lips on hers. "Are you home for the day?" *Home.* Maybe she shouldn't have said that.

"Can't go anywhere in this," he said about the storm.

She'd mentioned frying pork chops. Kane had nixed the idea because of the storm. He'd suggested something quick and simpler like grilled cheese sandwiches.

Darkness had descended early. The storm brewed loudly. Lightning flashed, thunder boomed overhead. Lights flickered.

"I hope I get this made before the power goes," she said about the soup that she'd had heating on the burner.

"Could happen." Sitting at the table behind her with Heather in his arms, he held the bottle for her.

Rachel slid the sandwiches onto plates. The scene was so close to perfect she felt a tightening in her throat. She couldn't afford to get sappy about this. But wasn't this what she'd always longed for the most? "The phone call was from Tracy Stevens," she said to dodge what might be foolish thoughts. "Tracy Jerick is her married name." She paused as she poured soup into bowls. "She invited us over to watch fireworks from her porch."

"Us?" As he patted Heather's back, she released a soft burp.

Rachel set a plate and bowl before him. "You, me and Heather," she said louder when thunder roared deafeningly.

He looked suddenly amused. "She didn't?"

"Kane, she was a friend of Marnie's, too." She meandered back to the stove to make sure she'd turned off the burners.

Puzzlement crept over his face. "I don't remember her."

"She had a really strict mother who was overprotective. Tracy hung around with us in school, but rarely went anywhere after school."

"Bet her parents wouldn't have been thrilled to learn she was hanging around with that Riley girl."

Rachel didn't argue. "Probably not." She perched on a chair across from him as he lowered Heather to the play yard. "But if it's all right that I take Heather there, we'll go while you're working."

He scowled at her. No other description fit the expression. "You don't have to ask. You take care of her better than a mother—" He stopped himself, then said, "You take good care of her."

How aware they were of certain words that might offend. "Thank you." Cautiously she spooned the tomato soup into her mouth and shared her latest news with him.

"So the baby wasn't your sister?"

Rachel shook her head. He had no idea how relieved she was about that, not that she would love Gillian any less. Her relief stemmed from not having to break such news to her sister.

Kane tapped his spoon at her bowl to get her attention. "Got another problem?"

One that she'd been mentally dodging because she'd been stymied about how to solve it. "Another half sister or brother lives somewhere. That person might not want to be found, have their life disrupted." How complicated life suddenly was. "Do you know anyone in town who's forty or older with the initials L.S.?"

His dark brows veed. "Offhand, no. But I don't know everyone. You need to talk to someone who knows everything. Like—"

"Velma?" Rachel had said the name in unison with him, drawing his grin. "I thought so, too." Lights flickered again. Rachel blew at the soup on her spoon and let her gaze meet his. "Do you want to go to bed early?"

"Might as well." His smile reached his eyes. "Before the power goes out."

Rachel called Velma the next morning. In response to questions about some woman named L.S., Velma said she knew no one. Of course, she asked the expected question. "Why do you want to know?"

"My mother indicated someone with those initials in her diary."

"L.S.? Hmm. Let me think about it."

Rachel had hoped Velma would provide a name. "Thanks," she said, a little disappointed.

"I'm glad you called. My cousin and her husband are coming to town around the Fourth of July. I told her about your jelly. And she'd like to buy some."

"Oh, she doesn't have to. I'd—"

"In my family, we pay for what we get," she said, sounding a touch insulted Rachel would suggest differently.

"Okay. I'll look forward to your visit." Rachel meant that. Though Velma was a bit stiff and prudish, she had a generous heart and had often dropped off fresh fruit for Rachel and had even brought a teddy bear for Heather. But Rachel admitted it required time and effort to get used to her, and the woman's attitude toward Kane annoyed her.

She made one more stop after the call, then met Tracy for lunch. They giggled their way down memory lane. Her high spirits from the luncheon lasted only until she reached the house. Alone, because Kane was on an all-night fishing trip, she couldn't avoid that phone call to her sister.

Gillian was elated with news. She'd been offered a modeling job with Lana Yang, the top fashion designer. With her sister's slim, modeling figure, long legs and high cheekbones, she'd be perfect for the designer who specialized in wedding gowns. "When is this happening?" Rachel asked.

"Two months. I'll have time to—wait, why are you so serious? Usually you're pumped up when I share good news."

Rachel told her everything, truly grateful Gillian wouldn't have to wonder if they were half sisters, if the mother she'd loved and grieved for hadn't been the one who'd given life to her.

"We need to find our brother or sister, don't we?" Gillian questioned without a moment's hesitation when Rachel had finished with her explanation.

"What?"

"Rachel, he or she has a family. Doesn't that person need to know that?"

Rachel remained silent, but she didn't like Gillian's idea, not one bit.

Aware of how close she was to letting depression sneak in, she looked for something to lift her spirits. Briefly, over another cup of coffee, she seesawed between buying a new outfit or getting her hair done. She really had no need for clothes, but her hair's uneven lengths and split ends demanded attention. Recalling the name of only one of the beauty salons, that's the one she chose. She made an appointment, certain Heather would sleep through the hair trim.

The local shop, Annie's Snip and Curl, a mecca for

gossip, was fairly empty because Rachel chose a noon
appointment. She was heading out when customers, a
few women she assumed were tourists since she
didn't recognize them, were wandering in.

She was glad she'd gone when Kane came home
that evening and suggested dinner at a local Italian
restaurant in the center of town.

From the moment they strolled into the restaurant
with its dark paneling, red-checkered tablecloths and
Tiffany lamps, people stared at them. Foolish and perhaps naive, Rachel had really thought that after the
fire, after Kane saved Mrs. Bensen that he'd be more
accepted.

"It bothers you, doesn't it?" he asked as they were
shown to a table near the wall of windows.

"Only for you."

He shrugged, making her wonder if he was really
so numb to it all.

"Your hair looks nice, Rachel." She watched his
gaze sweep over her face in a slow manner.

Even though she'd primped, pulling out of the
closet a white, scoop-necked dress with tiny blue
flowers, which followed her curves and flowed to her
ankles, his compliment surprised and pleased her.
She'd thought he might not notice. This was not a
man who often spoke soft words to a woman. "Thank
you."

In an unexpected move, he skimmed a fingertip
along her jaw to the tip of one strand. "Pretty."

Her eyes nearly closed with the tender touch. Even
when he wasn't near, she thought about him, about
caresses that made her senseless. In that second, with

his eyes staring at her, with his lips curved in a smile for her and the barest of his touch on her, she almost wished she could let herself believe. She'd told him she expected nothing. So why was she almost yearning for those promises?

While they placed orders, she sipped at her wine. Outside, with the Fourth of July two days away, the town was preparing for the big celebration. A red, white and blue banner was strung across Main Street. Flags waved in the wind from the flag holders in front of stores on the waterfront, preparations had begun for setting off the fireworks from one of the islands.

"What did you do today?"

Rachel laughed, fingered a few strands of her hair. "Besides this, I went to the town hall."

Despite questions in his eyes, Kane waited for the waiter to step away. "What did you expect to find there?"

"I didn't know if Velma would come through with an answer about L.S. She didn't." She'd felt obligated to learn all she could. "So I checked for a birth certificate under the name of Quinn besides ours. I didn't find one." She resumed her interest in her dinner. "It probably was a silly idea, but if someone could tell me something about the woman, it might help me look somewhere else."

"Hire a private eye."

Rachel shook her head and gave him a slim smile. "I couldn't afford that."

What she interpreted as exasperation swept over his face. "I could—"

"Please." Rachel couldn't accept that kind of help

from him. Didn't he understand? If she leaned on him in any way, she'd only feel drawn closer. "Don't say what I think you're going to say."

"I could," he returned predictably.

"No." Rachel looked down at the strong, tanned and callused hand closed over hers now and on the table between them. This was nice, comfortable. When younger, she used to fantasize about evenings like this, sitting at a candlelit table with someone special. Then she'd given up the fantasy. "I can't let you." Rachel slipped her hand from his as the waiter materialized with their dinner. "You work hard to make ends meet." Sometimes he worked sixteen hours a day.

"It'll get easier now." He offered her the basket of crusty bread. "I decided to let Lonnie take out the *Sea Siren* for me. So it and the *Maggie Lee* will be out at the same time. He likes playing captain."

She had to admit she was surprised. "It says a lot that you're trusting him with one of the boats."

"He told me today that he's done wandering and is staying in town for sure."

She sampled the lasagna on her plate before answering. "He's making a commitment?" She arched a brow, then at Heather's whimper, she cast a look at the baby in the infant seat on a chair beside her. "I thought he had a problem with that."

"Some old flame returned to town."

The power of love, Rachel mused. A dangerous power if a person relinquished their life to it.

Chapter Twelve

Feeling more content than she thought possible, she spent the next morning puttering around the kitchen. After dinner they'd walked along the waterfront under a star-filled sky. A comfortable silence had accompanied them. Kane had linked his hand with hers. How many times had she sat at her bedroom window, hoping for such a night with him? The evening had been so perfect. She hated to think about it ending, about there never being another. Without effort, he was touching her heart, making her wish a young girl's dream.

Rachel released a sigh at her own conflicting thoughts, then spent the next few minutes cleaning out the refrigerator. Afterward she thinned out her herb garden that had flourished on the north windowsill of the kitchen. Pleased with its progress, she was smiling when the phone rang.

The woman caller sounded to be around sixty, very responsible and a touch stern as she left a message for Kane. "The Hintley Employment Agency gave Mr. Riley's phone number to me," she said. "Please inform him that I have excellent references."

Rachel knew what she was feeling was silly. After all, she'd asked him to find a nanny. She jotted down the particulars that the woman rambled off to her and assured the woman that she would give Kane the message.

She should have been pleased. He'd done what she'd wanted him to do. But she hadn't liked the sound of the woman. No softness, no warmth. Would she hold Heather for no reason except that a baby needed the warmth and closeness of another body to feel loved?

Heather deserved someone who'd cuddle her and sing to her. She'd already lost her mother, had no father worth mentioning. For someone so young, so innocent, she'd been given a difficult path.

Kane could change that and make Heather's life as perfect and normal as possible. But even if he gave her everything she needed, that love and affection could be undermined by a cold, indifferent nanny.

Rachel wandered into Kane's den and kept herself busy working on her cookbook through the afternoon. Though no longer in a mood to meet Lori and her husband for a lobster broil, after cleaning up Heather and herself, she headed for the pier, anyway. She knew that not thinking too much might be best for her, but despite good company that evening and being stuffed and satiated, she was no less concerned. She made an excuse to Lori about being sleepy, promised to call her in the morning, then headed home.

By ten Kane came into the house. She considered mentioning the woman, but he'd been gone on another two-day fishing trip and looked so tired that Rachel expected him to shower, eat and drop into bed. He proved predictable, barely getting through the bowl of clam chowder without falling asleep.

Rachel locked the door and walked from the kitchen through the dining room to the short hall that led to bedrooms, turning out lights on her way.

Joining Kane in bed, she snuggled close, resting her face against his chest. As his arm tightened on her shoulder, she closed her eyes. Troubled thoughts about Kane, about that woman who called, about a sister or brother—a stranger—who was family, kept her awake for hours.

Those same thoughts awakened her before dawn the next morning. She prodded herself out of the bed, away from the comforting warmth of his body.

She gave thought to tearing the top paper off the notepad by the phone and throwing the woman's phone number away. Kane didn't have to hire her. There would be others, someone who sounded more gentle, more flexible. Someone who would view Heather's care as more than a job.

With that in mind she went to the kitchen. She plugged in the coffee brewer, but she merely glanced at the note. She had to trust Kane to do what was best for Heather.

With time to herself, she made the promised phone call to Lori and confirmed plans to meet her at the town square and watch the parade.

A cat meowing outside the back door detoured her toward the refrigerator. For the past week the stray cat, a calico, had made her home on the back porch. She'd shown up every morning since Rachel had given her that first bowl of milk.

"I think I'll call you Daisy," Rachel said, bending down to set a bowl on the wood porch. The cat undulated its back against her leg, tail high and swaying before she began lapping at the milk. Affectionately Rachel ran a hand over the cat's back, then left it alone and returned to the kitchen and the bacon she was frying. She nudged several slices of bacon and, with a glance at the clock, thought about rousing Kane.

"Fed that cat again, didn't you?"

She laughed at the sound of his voice close behind her. "I couldn't let her starve," she said in her defense.

With her turn to face him, he placed his hands at the curves of her waist. "She won't. She goes from house to house for handouts."

"Industrious cat," Rachel murmured, kissing his jaw as he craned his neck to see past her and into the frying pan.

"Something smells good."

"It's the bacon."

He nuzzled the side of her neck. "No. It's you."

Rachel laughed. As much as she would have liked to stay and enjoy the moments with him, the bacon demanded her attention.

''Whose phone number is this?'' he asked behind her.

She didn't need to look back to know he was holding the phone notepad. She wished now she'd gone with her first instinct and thrown the paper away. If that woman was the only one who answered the nanny's job, he'd have no choice except to hire her. ''A woman from the employment agency called about the nanny's job,'' she said, angrily shoving bacon around the pan with a fork.

Kane heard an edginess in her voice. With her back to him, he couldn't see her face, tell her mood. She wanted to leave soon. She'd said so. Yet he thought he heard something in her voice, something... *Knock it off.* She wanted to leave. Wasn't that why he'd called the employment agency right away? Hell, they both knew they couldn't go on like this. ''How did she sound?''

''Businesslike.''

A curt answer, a revealing one. She didn't like the woman, Kane deduced. If she had, she'd have shown more enthusiasm. She'd have tried to sell him on the woman, said something about how nice she sounded. She'd have wanted him to like her, too. ''I'll call her.''

Rachel couldn't keep quiet. That woman wasn't right for them. She angled a look at him, intending to state her case against the woman, but the sound of the doorbell kept her silent.

"Who'd be here so early?"

Rachel eyed the kitchen clock. The woman's timing was lousy. "That's Velma. She called yesterday and asked if she and her cousin could come over to buy the jelly."

"She's all yours." Kane was already on his way out of the kitchen. "I hear Heather," he said as an excuse, though the baby hadn't even whimpered.

Another, more impatient, jab at the doorbell sent Rachel into action and toward the front door.

From the moment Velma stepped in, loquacious as ever, she went on about her cousin's birthday. A full-figured woman like Velma, Doris Heppicutt reveled in Velma's attention and flattery and flashed a dimpled smile at Rachel.

"We want to buy several jars of your jelly. I told Doris and Bob," she said with a wave of a hand in the direction of Doris's husband, a tall, lanky, weathered-looking man in his fifties, who'd been noticeably silent, "that your jelly is the best I've ever tasted, and if you were staying here, I'd insist you enter the county fair. You'd get the blue ribbon for sure."

"Thank you, Velma." Rachel thought they would purchase the jelly and leave, but Velma plunked herself down on a kitchen chair to have a neighborly visit. Apparently Kane's timing was off for he reappeared with Heather in his arms. Because of the slight narrowing of his eyes as if he was in pain, Rachel guessed he'd assumed Velma would be gone.

"This is—" Velma paused, looked from him to Rachel as if stumped as to how to connect them. "Well, this is Kane Riley," she said, not bothering

to explain why the two of them were living together.
"And the baby is his niece. This is my cousin—"

"I remember you," Bob Heppicutt interrupted.
"We met a lot of years ago. Your boss called about
a new engine for his boat. We had the worst storm in
years that night. And you were hell-bent on getting
back home, but the sheriff had a roadblock up 'cause
the river was overflowing and roads had washed out."

Rachel rounded a look at Kane. She didn't need to
be a genius to guess what night the man was talking
about.

Kane responded with as few words as possible. "I
remember."

Rachel saw questions in Velma's eyes. Rather than
continue the conversation, Kane only nodded to the
man's question about whether he still had that boat,
then inched his way out of the room. To avoid her or
the truth? What was the truth? He'd barely left when
Velma asked the all important question. "Bob, was
his boss Charlie Greer?"

"I—" His brows knitted with his frown.

Rachel zeroed in on Velma's conversation with
Bob Heppicutt.

"Could be he mentioned his name," he was saying. "I couldn't say for sure though. But I'll tell you
the kid—he was a lot younger then—was worried sick
about his boss and almost desperate to get back. I
thought he was going to slug the sheriff and land in
jail. When he couldn't get through the roadblock, he
tried to make a phone call to someone, but the phone
lines were down. He kept mumbling, 'someone needs
to help him.' I remember that because the storm was

one of the worst we had, and power was out for two days. Do you know what he meant?''

Velma's eyes made contact with Rachel's. ''Yes, we do,'' Rachel answered.

Unbelievably Velma appeared at a loss for words.

''Are you ready to leave, Velma?'' her cousin asked.

Again, she merely nodded.

Rachel saw them to the door, thanked Doris for purchasing her jelly.

Though Velma's cousin stepped outside, Velma paused before Rachel. ''I'll take care of this,'' she announced. ''People need to know the truth.''

Rachel nodded, touched the woman's arm in a thank-you gesture, then closed the door. Velma wouldn't rest until she made amends, and finally others would realize how unfair they'd been to Kane.

Why, though, hadn't he told anyone what had happened? Before he left the house, she wandered into the den to talk to him. She paused in the doorway. Perched on the edge of the desk, he slanted a look at her as if he expected her questions. ''Why didn't you ever defend yourself, explain that you tried to come back?'' she asked.

Kane felt her reaching out to him. It was another step. If he took it, if he let her get inside him, he'd forget all that he needed to remember. He'd tell her that she was everything to him. He hadn't wanted her or Heather to be important to him.

''Kane?''

''It's not important.'' It hadn't mattered what the others thought, he could have told her. All that had mattered was that he'd lost the old man. All he'd had was Charlie. When he died, and with Marnie gone, there hadn't been anyone important enough to bother with.

Rachel sensed him trying to withdraw again. Despite intimacy and all they'd been sharing, he was still pushing her away. It hurt. It hurt more than she'd expected. And she knew why. *Oh, Rachel, you're such a fool.* She couldn't go on denying what she felt. She wanted to be a part of his and Heather's lives, love them.

"What happened then doesn't matter now."

As he stood, Rachel knew he'd leave. He'd said all he planned to about Charlie. She stepped away from the doorway to let him pass by. How quickly he emotionally isolated himself whenever he felt that he was getting too close to her.

She thought she knew why he did that. He claimed he didn't want to hurt her, but was that the real reason? She'd tried to shield herself, too. But she'd done it because caring for someone, loving them, was a risk. She'd believed if she had no husband, no children, she'd never have to give too much of herself, couldn't get hurt again.

But here she was fretting for Heather about who would nurture her, who would cheer her first step, her first word. And she was aching for Kane, wishing for a way to alleviate the pain and guilt he harbored within him. *Why* was suddenly easy to answer. Because she loved them. For her, love had come before with a slow, dreamy certainty, not with this suddenness, like a lightning bolt.

Oh, but it hadn't been sudden. It had been happening for weeks, hadn't it? She should have realized sooner. She'd seen such tenderness whenever Kane had touched Heather, had known only gentleness in his lovemaking.

But now what? She couldn't sit around, do nothing. A nanny was lurking nearby. If she couldn't make Kane see how much they belonged together, then they'd all lose.

Not having heard from him all day, Rachel wondered about his mood when he came in that evening. He looked tense. Was he expecting her to talk more about Charlie? She assumed he'd said all he wanted. He was consumed with a lot of pain for the man he viewed as father, friend, mentor. She didn't want to stir more. She gave him a smile, started to move toward him, but the phone rang.

"I'd like to speak to Kane Riley," a man said in response to her greeting.

Nearby, with Heather in his arms, Kane sent her a questioning look. "It's for you." She took Heather from him while he accepted the receiver.

"Angry at me?" he asked her despite the caller waiting for him.

No, I love you, Rachel wanted to say. "No, I'm not," she assured him and stepped back to give him privacy.

All day he'd mulled over how he'd left her that morning. All day it had bothered him more than he'd expected, more than he'd felt comfortable with. All day he'd been waiting, aching to see her smile. As she gave him one now, everything that had felt wrong seemed right. And he knew no matter how much he convinced himself that he didn't want her and the baby in his life, he did. He really did. On a silent oath at himself, he offered the caller a hello.

"I was told that you have Marnie Riley's baby," the voice said.

He straightened, tensed, consciously gripped the receiver tighter. "Who is this?" The name hadn't mattered to Kane. No DNA was needed. His gut clenched, told him that he was talking to Heather's father.

"My name is Ben Gaffney."

According to Rachel, he was the polite one, the guy who bought Marnie flowers, took her nice places. And didn't give a damn about her, Kane reflected. Stress jammed the muscles at his shoulders, spread up the back of his neck. Every protective instinct he possessed sprang forward for Heather. What if this guy wasn't the best for her?

"You're Marnie's brother, aren't you?"

He had heard no grief in the man's voice, no sorrow that his sister was gone. With effort Kane checked his anger. In fairness to the guy, he considered that Gaffney might have learned about Marnie dying long ago. No, that didn't wash. If that were true, he'd have called sooner about Heather. "That's right," he finally answered.

"I'm sorry about Marnie."

"What do you want?" Kane asked, struggling to keep his voice quiet. *Damn! Say why you called.* But he didn't need him to say: he was going to take

Heather. *This is what you wanted,* he reminded himself. Keeping her had never been an option. If he kept her, he might do something stupid—harm her, too. But how often did he think about Heather, about Rachel and her when he was away from home? How often did he stand by Heather's crib or want to feel the grip of those tiny fingers on one of his own?

"I was told that Marnie had the baby."

He'd been an idiot to buy the crib, decorate Heather's room. "Who told you that?"

"A mutual friend from the bank." He sounded annoyed at having to explain anything.

Gaffney knew about Heather and hadn't come. "How did you know where the baby was?"

"The friend—she said that a woman named Rachel Quinn had her, was bringing her to you."

Kane swore at himself. He was so damn stupid. Buying furniture, setting up a nursery. The baby was only supposed to be there temporarily.

Rachel's breath hitched. Even if she hadn't heard his words, she'd have known what was happening. He had that dark, brooding look again. She hadn't seen it in weeks. Before he set the telephone receiver back, she prepared herself for his words.

"That was Ben Gaffney." Briefly his eyes sliced to Heather. Then, as if shuttered, all emotion left them.

Her stomach knotted. *Ben Gaffney.* So he was the one. "He heard the baby was here."

It was hurting to breathe, she realized. "And he wanted...?"

Slowly he raised his eyes, met hers. The answer was in one look.

"He wants her, then?" Rachel asked.

"Rachel, why else would he be in town?"

Smarting warmth at the back of her eyes threatened tears. *Don't cry.* It would be dumb to cry. She had something more important to do. She had to convince him to keep Heather. "If Marnie wanted him to have the baby—"

"Rachel, he knows he's the father."

"Right." She held her ground, met his unflinching stare with a steady one. "And that means he must have known she was pregnant and he walked away."

Under his breath he muttered something earthy. "If that were true, he wouldn't be here now."

She held on to a hope that he'd misinterpreted the phone call. "Are you sure he wants Heather?"

"He has that right."

Of course he did. Hadn't Sean told her that, hadn't she known this was where it all would lead? Hadn't she agreed to stay until Kane located Heather's father? She'd hoped she would have convinced him by then that Heather belonged with him. She'd hoped he would feel as if he was losing a part of himself if he let her go. That hadn't happened yet.

She glanced at Heather, so small in the play yard he'd picked out for her. Briefly Kane's eyes met hers, then looked away. He must feel something for Heather. She couldn't be that wrong about him, couldn't believe he was that unfeeling. Something had started to happen between him and his niece. All they'd needed was a little more time. "Now what?"

He stared into space. Was he numbing himself to get through this? "Get her things together." His back to her, he stood at the window. "He asked me to meet him."

This wasn't supposed to be so hard, she told herself as she cradled Heather and rushed to the bedroom. Her throat tightened. She knew what Kane wanted her to do. Pack. She just couldn't. Not yet.

Keeping Heather close, she dropped to the rocker. How could he let her go? How could he willingly give her to another to raise when he was beginning to be the one Heather's eyes locked on when she looked around a room?

He thinks he's doing what's best for her. She knew that, but this wasn't. Stay calm, she berated herself. Pack her bag. Do something, anything.

She lowered Heather to her crib, but, needing one more second of contact, she placed a finger near Heather's tiny ones. Instinctively they curled around it. Oh, if only—

Don't go there, Rachel.

She slipped her finger from the little one's. Keep busy. Pack. Pack. She moved around the room from the dresser to a small bag on the bed as if she were playing some game to beat the clock. She couldn't linger. The faster she let go, the better off she'd be. But what about Heather?

"Is she ready?"

She would never be ready to let a child go. Not the baby boy she'd lost. And not this sweet baby girl. On a shaky breath, she faced him. "Yes. I'll bring the bag. You take her." She didn't dare hold her again.

As he bent over the crib, the heaviness in her chest grew. How could he do this? She really believed that Kane was best for Heather. *Tell the man to go away.* Fight for her, she wanted to yell. It was obvious that Kane cared about her. Heather was more his than that man's.

Her eyes swimming with tears, she trailed him out to the truck, waited while he locked Heather in her car seat, while he placed the play yard and portable crib in the truck bed. Everything was going except the furniture and the teddy bear lamp.

Standing at the truck door, he made a half turn toward her to take the diaper bag from her. "Rachel, this is best. She belongs with him."

Was he trying to convince himself or her? She backed up several steps, afraid he'd touch her, weaken her more. He was wrong. He was so wrong. She didn't answer, couldn't talk, couldn't allow herself one last look at the sweet baby inside the truck.

Chapter Thirteen

Without another word to him, Rachel dashed back up the porch steps and into the house. Even before she closed the door behind her, she heard the revving of the truck engine.

Inside, the silence was deafening. Mechanically she reentered the kitchen and dropped to the closest chair. It wasn't supposed to hurt like this. She wasn't supposed to care. She wasn't supposed to connect again with another child. But she had.

She folded her arms across her chest, tried to ease the pain within. She'd vowed not to let herself feel this way again. *You're such a fool. Didn't it hurt enough the last time?* Would she ever forget the emptiness she'd known when the doctor had stood by the bed, when he'd said, *Your baby is gone. I'm sorry.*

Was it the doctor who'd said those words. Or

someone else? A nurse? She didn't know. She couldn't remember. Maybe Keith. He'd never wanted the baby as much as she had.

Just like Kane. Or maybe he did and wouldn't let himself. He didn't think he deserved happiness or someone in his life. All Heather needed was love, she'd wanted to shout at him.

She swallowed hard against the threat of tears. She heard the ticking of the clock but couldn't move, didn't know how long she'd sat there. Words about accepting another baby that were in her mother's journal returned to her. "To refuse is unthinkable," she'd written. Rachel tugged the journal out of her purse and fanned pages until she reached the June 8 passage. Through blurry vision she stared at the words written in her mother's neat handwriting.

How could I not want the baby? What I can't understand is how the woman can give it up. Oh, what do I care? To have a baby in my arms again is to have prayers answered.

How like her mother. She would never turn away from a child. Oh, Mama. She let the tears roll down her cheeks. Mama, you know. You understand how it hurts to lose a child. Despite all efforts to keep detached whenever she'd held Heather, she'd wanted to bring her closer.

And now all she could do was pack, leave. With effort, she pushed herself to her feet. She'd taken only one step toward the doorway when she heard the hum of the truck engine.

At the unexpected sound, she cast a quick glance at the kitchen clock. She couldn't have been sitting so long. She'd wanted to be packed and ready to leave when Kane returned.

With the back of her hand she brushed away tears. Now even this would be harder. Wasn't it bad enough that she'd been forced to say goodbye to one of them? She had to leave quickly. No more tears. At least not now, not until she was alone again.

"I forgot to give you the carriage," she said, making herself head his way when she heard the closing of the front door. Her steps faltered. Her heart hammered. "Kane." She spoke his name but couldn't take her eyes off Heather. Wrapped in the lightweight yellow blanket, she was asleep in his arms. "You still have her." She wouldn't do well, Rachel knew. She couldn't let go of Heather twice without breaking down. "Is he picking her up later?"

"She's not going anywhere."

What had he said? Her head snapped up. "What?"

"He doesn't want her."

"Oh, my God." She didn't remember moving. Arms out, she gathered Heather to her breast, caressed the soft dark hair, kissed her velvety soft cheek. "Did he see her?" she asked, fighting herself to keep from holding Heather too tightly.

"I met him outside the Triple A Motel where he's staying. He said, 'I'm not taking her.'"

She supposed she was being naive, but disbelief rushed her. "How can he not want her?" Rachel stared down at Heather's sweet little face. "She's so special."

"He was pretty cut-and-dried." His jaw tightened. "He said he hadn't had anything to do with Marnie since that one night." Rachel noted he repeated the man's words as if they'd left a bitter taste in his mouth. "He told me that he didn't want the baby. Had no intentions of taking her." An unmistakable edge of anger deepened his voice. "He didn't even want to know her name."

"Did you tell him that she's his responsibility?" She only asked the question because she assumed that's what he would say. After his own father's failure to act responsibly, Kane would believe that.

"I didn't bother."

She was confused now. "You didn't?"

"Why should she go where she isn't wanted?" Kane gave his head a slow shake as if still coming to terms with what had happened. "He told me if I took him to court to prove paternity, if I wanted money, it wouldn't matter. He wasn't going to take her. He wouldn't let her disrupt his life."

Rachel said what she was thinking. "She's better off without him." But now what? She almost dreaded what his next words would be.

Her attention returned to him as he slipped a folded paper from his shirt pocket. "He'd made sure there wouldn't be a 'problem'. He went to a lawyer, got a paper drawn up relinquishing all rights to her."

Rachel snuggled Heather closer. Where would Heather go if no one wanted her?

"I'm going to keep her, Rachel."

I'm going to keep her. Over and over the words circled in her mind. Stunned, she simply stared at him, wondered if she was gaping. Was that a snap decision or had he thought long about it?

"I don't know if I'm doing her any favors. There's a good chance I'll do her more harm than good, but she's family. I wasn't there for Marnie. There's nothing I can do about that except be around for her baby."

"Oh, Kane." She closed the space between them. A myriad of emotions fluttered through her. She didn't try to sort through them. The only one that mattered was her happiness for Heather. Rachel said a silent prayer of thanks, then coiled an arm around Kane's neck. "I was worried that—"

"I'd hand her over to Social Services?" He placed a hand at her hip.

Rachel hadn't wanted to believe that, but the possibility had existed. Knowing his feelings about getting close to anyone, she considered the notion that he might think Heather would be better with them than him.

"I wouldn't," he assured her. "She's got family."

She smiled, pleased with the way everything had gone. "We need to celebrate." She kissed him quick but hard before stepping away. "Let me put Heather to bed first."

She rushed out with Heather, only to return within minutes. Content, delighted at what had happened, she laughed softly when she joined him at the counter.

He swung away from the opened door of the refrigerator with the bottle of wine in his hand. "What's funny?"

"I was thinking how different this day is now. I

thought Heather would be gone this evening, and here we all are. Because of you.'' Pressing herself against him, she snaked an arm around his neck. ''Have I told you that you're my hero.''

''Oh, stop,'' he grumbled, but a hint of a smile crinkled faint lines at the corners of his eyes.

Raising her face to his, she stroked the hair at the nape of his neck. ''Let me prove it to you.'' Had she felt so alive before? she wondered as his mouth closed over hers. Others had slipped in and out of her life. Others she'd had no trouble forgetting. Desire humming through her, she glided her hands over his strong, broad back.

She'd never thought of herself as a romantic, but every touch, every kiss with him seemed magical. As he raised his mouth from hers, she stared into eyes clouded with passion—for her. Then he lifted her into his arms. Against her, she felt the hard beating of his heart.

''Grab the glasses.'' He stopped at the counter long enough for her to snatch up the wineglasses.

Rachel laughed, felt the cold bottle in his hand against her back. But the rest of her body was warm, anticipating.

At the bed he slowly lowered her feet to the ground. ''Give me those.'' He took the glasses from her, set them and the bottle on a bedside table.

''I want to drink the whole thing,'' she said a little giddy already.

''Tomorrow you'll be sorry,'' he murmured against her throat.

''That's tomorrow.'' Standing between his spread

legs, she tugged at his shirt. "All I care about is to-night." For a little while she didn't want to think about anything except him.

In one swift move he yanked the shirt over his head. With a kiss, a caress, he could make her mind-less. Desire sweeping through her, she pressed her lips to his broad chest, to the hard, warm flesh. He felt wonderful. Strong, sleek, muscular. Her mouth on his again, she felt a sweet pang of longing. She wanted forever. Her heart, her soul belonged to this man and the child in the other room.

As kisses deepened, he touched her with a tender-ness that spoke volumes, a tenderness that bound them despite words insisting on no ties. Caresses grew demanding. His mouth moved everywhere, his voice grew ragged as he cursed their clothing.

Need, not want, controlled her. So much had seemed wrong hours ago. Yearning, she closed her eyes. Naked, they flattened their bodies against each other, and as he pressed his hardness to her, she melted into him to feel every inch of the length of him against her.

With his mouth on hers, she didn't remember the move onto the bed. Arms wrapped around him, she held on almost desperately, longing for the mindless haze to sweep over her.

As his knuckles grazed skin at her inner thigh, she threw back her head, pressing it into the pillow be-neath her and closed her eyes. She was a creature of sensation. Her skin warmed. Her body tingled. When he inched his way down, spreading kisses over her belly to her thigh, he took her to the edge of sense-lessness.

Her hunger matching his, she kissed his chest, his belly, lowered her head to trace the fine dark line of hair with her tongue. Beneath her slightest touch, his muscles rippled. With a caress of her mouth or a stroke of her tongue, his body tensed. With his groan of pleasure, with his shudder, he gave her the power.

On a heady sigh, he whispered her name, tugged her to him, kissed her again, hard and full. Strong, muscular thighs pressed against soft ones, and with a moan that echoed hers, they rolled on the bed.

Before she took another breath, he brought her beneath him. A sound, urgent and no more than a breathy whisper slipped from her lips as she opened her body to him. A fierceness they hadn't shared before took over. They came together, straining against each other. Mindless to everything but him, she took him even deeper into her, filling herself until flesh melded, until they blended as one. And as if this moment might be their last, she gave him everything she possessed.

In brighter spirits than she'd been in days, Rachel met Lori at the town square next morning. A crowd that stood shoulder to shoulder lined the town's main street for the annual Fourth of July parade. The day was meant to be carefree and lighthearted.

"Remember that, Rachel?" Lori asked, pointing at one of the floats. "It looks like the float we worked on." A giggle rose in her voice. "What a disaster that was."

The memory of the badly constructed float stirred Rachel's laugh. "I remember," she said, and from her position, sitting beside Lori at curbside, she craned her neck to see the next float, to forget some things she couldn't do anything about. At least not right now.

For the next hour, float after float from community services and different high school clubs passed by. Heather slept through it all, mainly because Rachel covered her ears with her hands to keep her from being startled whenever the school bands marched by with horns blaring and drums pounding.

Rachel admired the last float, one decorated with red carnations, white mums and blue forget-me-nots that depicted the signing of the Declaration of Independence with high school students in wigs and period garb standing around a table. While the float glided past spectators, not wanting to get caught with Heather in a crush of people, Rachel suggested to Lori that they ease their way through the crowd while they could.

"I'm off to join Matt's family," Lori said when they got clear of the town square. She talked about her in-laws in what sounded like a forced breezy tone. "They make enough of their own fireworks all the time. Have fun at Tracy's," she added on a departing note.

Rachel negotiated Heather's carriage toward the ocean and in the direction of a cove where Tracy Jerick lived. She paused, was regarding a painting of a seascape in one of the gallery windows when she heard someone call her name.

Velma scurried toward her, not even bothering with a quick hi. "I was talking with my cousin after we left you. She remembered a woman whose initials were L.S.," she said, indicating that she'd talked to others about what Rachel had said. Rachel had expected as much and wasn't offended. If she got information, she didn't mind being the topic of the day for the gossips.

"The woman's name was Lenore Selton."

Rachel felt her heart thudding against the wall of her chest. "Lenore Selton."

"Yes. My cousin taught at the high school years ago. Well, she's been retired more than twenty years, but she recalled a science teacher at the high school by that name. She didn't know for certain that Lenore knew your mother, but she assumed they met at some faculty function since your father taught at the same school."

Everything she was saying made sense.

"Velma, wait up." Margaret Bensen rushed her steps to join them.

Rachel would have preferred to keep their conversation private, but she needed to act as if she and Velma were merely passing time, and keep everyone's suspicions at bay.

"I never thought of asking you," Velma said to Margaret. "She worked at the high school," Velma informed Rachel.

"In the cafeteria," Margaret said. "Kids in those days had a diet of French fries and chocolate milk. I don't know what they eat now."

"We were talking about Lenore Selton," Velma cut in before Margaret could go on.

"Oh, I knew her." And with those words, Margaret shared every smidgen of information she had about Lenore Selton.

With plenty of time before the evening's festivities, Rachel ambled past other art galleries near the dock and along the plank walkway to the slips. Several boats had been anchored there. Now, with sunset, almost all of them were piloting out to sea for a spectacular view of the island and the fireworks display. Tourists had poured into town. Everyone was in a celebrating mood. On the beach people had started lobster broils and volleyball games. Huge umbrellas were plunked down, and children played tag in the sand or built sand castles.

Rachel wanted to talk to someone. Not someone—Kane. That was logical, she reasoned. No one else knew about her search. Admitting her father's unfaithfulness was too hard to share with Lori or Tracy. Kane was the only one who knew everything.

She pushed Heather's carriage around a souvenir stand. A light breeze whipped at canopies over store windows, the warm air carried the smell of the ocean.

In a nearby slip Lonnie was fussing around on the touring boat. It had a large interior cabin with windows and an abundance of chairs and benches on the outer deck where everyone would crowd to watch the fireworks. While the owners of touring boats took care of last-minute preparations for the evening's cruise along the coast and an ocean's view of the fireworks, a gathering had already begun on land.

From the pier Rachel watched Kane coming in with the fishing boat. It gleamed beneath the setting sun. The boat's hull tore through the water. Wearing a gray T-shirt, worn-looking, faded jeans and a captain's hat, he stood at the wheel. On the deck several men, sitting in the boat's fighting chairs, laughed and swigged beer. Behind the boat a gull skimmed the water in search of food.

As he brought the bow closer to the pier, sunlight reflected off chrome. Enthusiastically the men on the boat waved to a couple and a woman waiting at the dock.

"Hey," Kane called out to her from the deck. Puzzlement deepened lines in his face as he climbed the stairs to join her. "I thought you were going to your friend's house to watch the fireworks."

"Tracy Jerick's home. I am going there, but I went to see the parade." Because it seemed right, she leaned close, brushed her lips across his cheek. He smelled of the sea, held the taste of the salty spray on his face. She waited for him to say something. Water lapped against the pier. Her heart hammered. Was that too public to suit him? She doubted anyone had really noticed.

"That was nice, but I'd guess you came for another reason."

Why could he read her so well when she had such a difficult time understanding his moods and what did or didn't please him? "I wanted to tell you that I ran into Velma. Her cousin knew L.S."

"L.S.? *The* L.S.?"

"Yes." Nearby, on the tour boat's deck, Lonnie

was welcoming customers for their cruise. ''Velma
supplied a name. The woman was a science teacher.
Lenore Selton. And according to Velma's cousin and
Margaret Bensen, who worked at the school, too, Lenore was a really nice lady.''

He took off his cap and set it on the canopy of
Heather's carriage. Beneath the sunlight his hair
gleamed as dark as a raven's feathers. ''That dis-
pleases you?''

There was no way to explain her feelings without
sounding less than admirable. ''I wanted to be told
that the woman was a witch,'' she said honestly. At
that moment she realized how much she trusted him
and willingly shared feelings with him. The truth was
that she'd wanted reasons to hate Lenore Selton. Instead Margaret had raved about Lenore, ''a pretty brunette whose coppery hair shone like gold beneath sunlight,'' she'd said.

Though Rachel's mother's hair had been a soft
blondish-brown, her father's had been auburn. Sean's
was the same color. Gillian's was a brighter red, while
Rachel's shone more blond among the red strands. ''I
wonder what color hair the child had? Isn't that ridiculous?'' She gritted her teeth at her own thought.
''I hate this. I don't want to wonder about that person.
And I don't want to know about him or her.''

Hearing the anger in her voice, she drew a deep
breath. She couldn't curb a bitterness within her. She
didn't want to meet her half sister or her half brother.
Every time she thought about that sibling, all her il-
lusions about her father shattered again. ''I don't want
to look for the person,'' she admitted.

"The person being…?"

"My father's illegitimate child. Gillian thinks we should do that. And look for Lenore Selton, too." She appealed to Kane, though what he thought wouldn't matter. The decision had to be made by Gillian, Sean and herself. "What would be gained? That person would be a reminder. Every time I looked at him or her, I'd remember that my father had an affair." She supposed she sounded uncaring to him. But then he was so weighed down with guilt about Marnie, could he see her side of this? "You don't understand, do you?"

"It's not my place," Kane said, but he didn't understand how Rachel, someone so loving, so generous, could turn her back on one of her own. That person had done nothing wrong.

Rachel sent a glance in Lonnie's direction. "They're ready to leave, Captain," she said, obviously straining for a smile.

Kane didn't want to leave her. He could tell she was miserable. She shouldn't be alone. *Right,* he mused. *And she shouldn't be with you.* He'd done a poor job of remembering that, even as he'd tried to maintain distance from both of them.

Concern accompanying her, Rachel wandered back to town to Benny's Café for his Fourth of July special, a barbecued beef dinner with fries and corn on the cob.

As nightfall came, more people swarmed into town. By eight o'clock the town's populace and a throng of tourists were crowding the beaches and rocky coastlines. Everything from lobster boats to yachts bobbed in the choppy water.

Rachel sat with Tracy on her home's front porch. On a cliff along the rocky coastline, the Cape Cod boasted a panoramic view of the ocean and several islands.

With darkness coming, the sky burst alive with color—blue, red, green and pink sprays that resembled the branches of a willow tree, or silver and gold sunbursts or gigantic mums. Endlessly the display of showy lights went on. More colors exploded above them—pink and orange, blue and green swam together. Distant and faint cheering and clapping filled the night air.

"Is she all right?" Tracy questioned about Heather.

Rachel looked away from the sprays of colors falling toward the black water. "She's fine."

"I don't know why I'm surprised that she's such a beautiful baby. Marnie had such great looks—dark Irish." Her expression turned pensive. "I thought—"

With her sudden silence, Rachel gave up her interest in a glittering gold and silver sunburst. "You thought what?"

"That she would get what she wanted." Rachel supposed she looked puzzled because Tracy added, "Don't you remember?"

Another riot of color blazed the sky. More shouts of appreciation followed. Rachel watched the lights fall toward the water for only a second, but her attention shifted to what Tracy was saying, to what Rachel should have remembered.

Learning the truth carried a lot of pain sometimes, she decided a moment later. Who knew that better than her. To tell Kane about his sister might alleviate his guilt, but it would also hurt him.

Chapter Fourteen

Early-morning sunlight cast the bedroom in a soft, hazy glow. Kane had left before sunrise, not giving her a chance to talk to him. She was still fretting, wondering if it wasn't best to say nothing.

So much guilt shadowed him because of his beliefs about Marnie. After years of caring for her, he couldn't get past feelings that he'd let her down when she needed him. Of course, that wasn't true. But he would never believe her no matter how hard she tried to convince him.

Rachel dropped to the window seat in Heather's room with its view of the rocky coastline and the bay. Lobster boats glided over the water as they came in. She stared with unseeing eyes at them now as she mulled over her problems.

In his mind, he'd failed to be somewhere when two

people needed him. Only he could ease the pain fes-
tering within him. But wasn't her silence about Marnie the same kind of omission of truth that she'd de-
clared her parents guilty of? She had no choice. She
had to tell Kane what she'd learned about Marnie's
last days in Hubbard Bay.

The late-afternoon chill in the air was unusual for
July. Leaves rustled beneath a brisk wind. Bundling
Heather in a lightweight blanket, Rachel left the
house and ambled toward the dock. She could have
driven, but needed thinking time, a way to say everything right.

"Rachel?"

At the sound of Velma's voice, she wanted to keep
walking. She couldn't believe that twice in twenty-
four hours Velma was stopping her.

"Rachel, there's something I need to say." The
distress threading Velma's voice garnered Rachel's
attention. "I've been trying to decide if I should tell
you this. I mean, it was so long ago that I didn't know
if you knew. At least I didn't until you mentioned
Lenore. Then I figured you probably knew about
her."

Rachel couldn't handle discussing her family secrets and making them tomorrow morning's gossip.
"Velma, I don't want to—"

"This won't go anywhere." Softly Velma said the
assurance as if she was worried someone might hear.
"I've known this since you were a little girl and never
said anything to anyone."

"You knew about Lenore?"

"Oh, yes. I'm sorry that I didn't admit that right away." Discomfort rushed into her eyes. "It wasn't my place, and well—your mother and I were good friends. Out of loyalty to her, I always kept her secrets. I guess you learned about your father and Lenore."

"I read about it in my mother's diary."

"Your mother was a wonderful woman, but she had problems. You know that, don't you?"

"She had a nervous breakdown."

"Yes, after she lost the baby. She just couldn't cope." Only sympathy laced her voice. "I felt so bad for you and little Sean, for your father. He loved her."

Rachel had thought that. But a man doesn't love one woman and have an affair with another.

"I don't think I ever saw a man so heartbroken as he was when they lost the baby. He sat in the hospital waiting room and sobbed. Then he went in to see your mother, and she was lost to him, too. It took her so long to find her way back to him. He needed someone. I'm not making excuses for him. I don't abide by people breaking their marriage vows. But you need to know that the doctor said your mother might never get well. She was catatonic for a while, Rachel."

"Oh, my God." She hadn't been aware of the severity of her mother's mental illness. "I didn't know that."

"When you mentioned L.S., I was afraid that you'd heard about your father's affair, and believed the worst of him."

How could she not? "I had."

"Don't." Velma, sometimes petty and definitely

gossipy, surprised Rachel. She was seeing a different side of her, one filled with compassion. "He truly never would have done anything to hurt your mother. He reached out to Lenore during some of the most difficult days of his life. I think Lenore knew that, too. He was so full of remorse because of the affair."

"How do you know this?"

"I know the affair didn't last long. And he was living between the house, with you and your brother and the hospital, with your mother, even when she didn't know he was there. So I know that the affair ended almost immediately."

"My mother was going to take Lenore's baby."

"Yes," she confirmed. "She was. Your father had told her about the affair. Mary Ann sat in my kitchen and told me. For months she hadn't been a wife to him. She said that she loved him and forgave him."

"Was that when she told you about the baby?"

"No. Later. I couldn't understand how she could take the child. But she said the child, any child was a gift from God."

One to love and treasure, Rachel mused.

"But she told me that Lenore changed her mind," Velma added. "She was a highly intelligent woman, but acted scattered sometimes. Her whole family was smart. I believe she had a sister—Edith—who was a professor, and taught at a university somewhere." She frowned, aware she'd strayed from what Rachel wanted to know. "I know your father never meant to betray your mother. He was grieving for two people, his child and his wife."

And had reached out to someone else. While he'd

done that, Kane's father had shut everyone out. What was worse? "Velma, thank you." She could imagine how difficult that time had been for her father. The love of his life hadn't even recognized him.

"I wanted you to know."

Rachel touched her hand affectionately. She felt a peace of mind she hadn't known since the day she opened her mother's diary, read those words about her father's affair. "I understand better." A lot of things. And she felt even more determined now to talk to Kane, make him listen, really listen to her.

The moment she reached the weathered pier, she spotted him coming out of the bait shop. Rachel would have preferred a more private place to have a conversation with him. Instead of moving closer, she waited near the end of the dock, away from the boats. She knew when he'd noticed her.

Squinting against the sunlight, his eyes narrowed even more with a frown while he closed the distance between them. "Something's wrong?"

"Nothing," Rachel was quick to assure him. "Except I don't think you should hire that woman," she blurted out. "She won't be right for Heather."

"Rachel." His brows pinched. He looked as if she was forcing him to reconsider a decision he'd already made. "I don't have a lot of choices."

"I'll stay." There she'd said it.

Was it her imagination or had his back straightened in the manner of someone preparing to face difficulty? "I know you're willing to—"

"Permanently."

Slowly he raised his eyes to meet hers. Rachel held

her breath. Nothing registered on his face to indicate he was happy with her announcement.

"That's not a good idea."

Mentally she'd prepared for a little opposition. "I want to stay."

"Rachel, I haven't changed my mind. I don't want a woman in my life." Kane watched her wince. He hadn't planned to cut so deeply, but it seemed this was the only way. "You knew that from day one. I told you that. You told me you accepted everything."

She lifted her chin as if she was daring him to take a poke at it. "I was wrong."

"What's changed?"

"I love you now." As the wind tossed her hair forward, Rachel tucked strands behind her ear. "That's what's changed." When a woman gave herself to a man who didn't want to give anything back, she was destined for heartache if he was unfeeling and insensitive. But Kane wasn't. He was a giving, caring man. "I don't need you to explain why you feel the way you do. I know what you believe. Whenever you love someone, you hurt them. That's what this is really all about, isn't it?"

"It's the truth."

"That's not the truth," she countered. "Some unfortunate things have happened, but you're not the reason for them."

"Yeah, I am," he said, flaring. "The problem was I forgot that. I'd be with you and not want to remember. But I can't keep doing that." As she started to shake her head at the nonsense of his words, he framed her face with his hands and stilled her. "I thought I was making the right decision to leave my sister for the job. I was wrong. And in the end look what happened to Marnie. If I'd stayed, if I'd been there for her, she'd have never left town. She'd have never met Gaffney. And this wouldn't have happened. And I did the same thing with Charlie. I'm not going to do something like that to you.''

''Listen to yourself. Really listen. If all that were true, Heather wouldn't exist. Do you really believe that would have been better?'' His hands dropped away from her. He looked ill suddenly. She knew she was hitting hard but he needed to start seeing people, himself the way he really was.

''You can twist this any way you want, but that doesn't change anything. People I care about get hurt. Dammit, why don't you leave now? If you stay, I'll hurt you. I can't love you, love anyone.''

''Because you don't care about Heather, about me?''

''Rachel, this is pointless.''

''I'm glad you're not denying it, because I see love in your eyes every time you hold Heather.'' She had to make him understand, and in that second she sensed it was now or never. For some people, like his father, time didn't always take away the pain. The hurt grew, became so strong that there was no room to love anyone else. She couldn't let him be one of those people. ''I know you do care. And what do you know? Amazing, isn't it?''

He heaved a sigh. ''What?''

''You care, and Heather is still okay, isn't she?''

''Don't do this,'' he nearly whispered, putting only

inches between them, as two couples, laughing, squeezed by on the walk. "This won't do any good."

Rachel spoke softly. "You have to realize that you're not responsible for Marnie's actions, for her impulsiveness or for what happened to her."

"I am. I let my sister down. And she's dead," he said low as if angry for having to say the words aloud. "She relied on me to be near for her, and I wasn't, Rachel."

She wished for more privacy but didn't dare suggest that they move. If she stopped now, he wouldn't listen to more. "I can't believe you've burdened yourself with so much unnecessary guilt. People who knew her said she did exactly what she wanted to do."

His gaze clashed with hers. "You don't think I knew her?"

"She loved you, Kane. I think she'd say whatever would make you happy."

"What do you know about us?"

"All along Marnie planned to leave. She told Tracy and Lori," she added. After Tracy had told her about Marnie, Rachel had called Lori to get verification, to make sure Tracy hadn't just been gossiping. "Marnie told both of them that she was leaving as soon as she could. When you left town, Tracy came to the house, saw that Marnie had a suitcase packed. Your sister was planning to call you, tell you she wanted to come to Florida. But it didn't matter what you said. She was taking the first bus out of here."

His head reared back slightly. "No, she didn't."

Rachel made herself go on. "She told Tracy that

she'd been looking for an excuse to leave. 'As long as Kane was here, I couldn't go,' she'd said. That would have hurt you. Only you had kept her in Hubbard Bay. Without you around, she felt no connection to anyone. But with you in Florida, she wouldn't have to face you. She could do what she wanted. She felt free to leave. All the guilt you felt was unwarranted. You weren't responsible for her leaving. She'd have gone eventually, anyway.''

He shifted his stance, stared past her with unseeing eyes as if viewing something in his mind's eye.

''Kane, she constantly told Lori and Tracy that she'd planned to leave. She hated it here. I remember her saying that she wanted to get away from the smell of fish. She wanted excitement.'' Marnie had said more. She'd complained about how boring Hubbard Bay was. She'd wanted everything she didn't have. She'd wanted money, nice clothes, to find a rich man. She'd laughed and said he could be young or old. She didn't care. She wasn't marrying for love.

''I thought you were smarter, Rachel.'' Squinting against the sunlight, his eyes slitted. ''This is nothing but gossip.''

She had to endure his anger. The truth was more important. ''I'm telling you what she told me.'' She couldn't back down. ''At any time when living in Texas, Marnie could have come home, returned to you. Isn't that true? It was her decision not to come home.'' Before she lost courage to say everything, Rachel kept going, hoping she could get through to him. He needed to realize that he wasn't any more responsible for the way Marnie's life went than he was for Charlie's death. "Charlie sent you out of town to get the engine. You didn't cause the storm, put up the roadblock, choose not to come back. What happened that night wasn't your fault. No one is responsible for another person's actions."

"You talk a good game, Rachel."

"What does that mean?"

"The child isn't responsible for what your father did, but you don't want any part of the brother or sister you could have, do you?"

Rachel swayed slightly, stunned by his challenge, by the truth in his words. Mentally she shook aside the gnawing realization trying to close in on her. She needed to concentrate on him, only him. "Kane, please, listen to me. I love you."

He whipped away as if her words annoyed him. Rachel's heart ached for him. She stared at his back, rigid and tense. "I don't know what else to say." Sadness weaved through her as she considered how much they'd lose because he couldn't reach out for her, because she didn't know how to reach him. "You're wallowing in guilt. You only see yourself, your guilt about the people who are gone. What about the people living who love you? Don't they count, too?"

She took a step away, paused, hoping he'd turn around, stop her. But when she looked back, her heart twisted. He was already boarding the boat.

After all that Kane had said, by the time Rachel entered the house, she realized she couldn't stay.

Whether he loved her or not, the possibility existed that he would never admit it even if he did.

She started to pack, but as she wandered into the nursery with its teddy bear wallpaper, her heart grew heavier. All she wanted to do was sit and hold Heather. Now that she'd accepted how much she loved them, how would she let go of them?

"You're such a sweetheart," she murmured, kissing Heather's soft cheek. Who would take care of her after she left? Children were so precious. Her mother had known that. Unlike her, Rachel had been afraid to accept another baby in her life, to love it.

While talking with Kane, trying to make him realize he wasn't responsible for someone else's actions, she faced a truth of her own. The child from her father's affair wasn't responsible either for anything that had happened. She knew now that somewhere a sister or brother existed, and maybe Gillian was right—they did need to find that person, make him or her a part of their family.

She wasn't surprised Kane had tossed a challenge at her. She remembered the look on his face when she'd told him that she'd wanted no part of the child her father had from an affair. She'd known he hadn't understood. She'd known—

One thought died as another took hold. Oh, what if the problem still existing between them was her fault? She'd rejected the idea of accepting a child from her father's affair. Was her rejection of that sister or brother part of the reason why Kane really wouldn't let himself love her? Was he afraid to believe in love between them?

He had such sad memories of his father, must have believed that in his sorrow his father had abandoned Marnie and him. From his father he'd learned that loving someone too much meant getting hurt.

He didn't understand, she realized now. He would never have had such doubts if she hadn't held back her love for so long from him and Heather. But she hadn't wanted to give too much of herself to anyone again. She'd been afraid to love him and Heather, take that risk.

Kane worked so hard scrubbing the deck sweat poured off him. He finished, cleaned out the bucket, then washed up in the head on the boat. She loved him. Damn. He'd never expected Rachel to say those words.

An ache spiraled through him. He shrugged his shoulders trying to slough away the pain within. Standing at the boat's stern, he stared into the dark water. He'd said some hard things to her, had watched the light leave her eyes, but he had wanted to protect her. He knew how love destroyed. It had ruined his father, changed him from a loving father into a drunk. He hadn't wanted to experience the same torment his father had. He hadn't wanted to love Rachel and Heather. He hadn't wanted to hurt.

He swayed as his own words slammed back at him. *He hadn't wanted to hurt.* Dammit. He cursed himself. Who was this really about? All this time had he been fooling himself? Was this about him not her? Was he the one he'd been really trying to protect?

He stared out at the water, trying to make sense of

everything. He'd seen what love had done to his father. He'd lost his mother, then him. Every person he'd ever cared about he'd lost. Deep inside him, fear had grown, he realized. He hadn't wanted to lose anyone else.

In the kitchen Rachel stared out the window at the gray sky. Before tears started, she picked up the receiver to punch out her sister's phone number. She'd tell her all that she'd learned about Lenore. Perhaps she'd visit her for a few days.

The sound of the back door opening stilled her. Her pulse hammering, she placed the phone in its cradle, then turned to face him. Had he come to tell her to get out?

As he stared at her with such serious eyes, she drew a deep breath, trying to prepare herself for those words. Wasn't this the real chance she'd taken? All along she'd known she could be hurt. She'd known the risk to her heart from the first moment she'd picked up the baby, answered Kane's kiss. She'd known that the more time she was with them, the harder it would be to let go. And still she had stayed. She shifted her stance as his eyes remained on her. "Do you want me to leave now?" she asked, wishing again for some way to reach him.

Slowly he shook his head, closed the door behind him. "I didn't say that."

Emotion flooded her with longing. She wanted to rush to him, feel his arms around her. With effort, she stayed where she was. "You wish I hadn't said what I did, don't you?"

"I wish—" he gave his head another shake "—I wish everything had been different."

It took effort but she relied on a strength that before had gotten her through some devastating events. "Different how?"

"I wish I'd told you what I felt before this, how much I love you."

Pressure in her chest made breathing suddenly difficult. *Love me. He loves me.*

"Say something."

She hadn't thought she could love him more, but her heart filled with it. "I don't—I don't know what to say." She took a step, made the first move to close the distance between them, end the terrible emptiness she'd felt since leaving him.

"Then I'll talk." A frown etched deeply in his face. "When earlier you said that you loved me, I'd wanted to drag you close, tell you I loved you, too. I held back."

Longingly she swept her gaze over him. He looked different, she realized now. At peace, happier. "I understand. I know you thought you needed to protect us."

"I wish I were that noble," he muttered self-deprecatingly. "That's what I wanted to believe. But it was myself." Close now, he reached out, fingered a few strands of hair near her cheek. "I wouldn't let myself love you because I didn't want to lose you. Sounds dumb, doesn't it?"

"Not to me. For so long, fear kept me from admitting how much I wanted both of you," she said, amazed how mistaken they both had been.

"You had more courage." She released a small sigh as he slipped his arms around her. "It took me longer to realize that. Then when you walked away today, I knew you were going to leave, really leave. It didn't matter that I hadn't told you I loved you." He gave his head a slow shake as though dumbfounded by his own actions. "Because you were in my heart, and when I lost you, I'd ache as if part of me was gone."

She swallowed hard against the knot in her throat. "I'll never leave." She set a hand to his chest, felt the hard, quick beat of his heart, then brought her mouth to his again. This time the kiss was filled with sweetness and a promise of more, and with all the love she'd prayed for. Slowly, reluctantly his lips lifted from hers. Rachel longed to merely feel and ignore problems, but one was too important to disregard. "About children—"

"Rachel." A softness, a tenderness she'd never heard before hung in his voice. "We have a family." Gently he caught the back of her neck. "We have Heather. And we can adopt. You're such a wonderful mother already to Heather."

Rachel couldn't let him make light of something that would affect their whole lives. "Kane, you'll want children of your—"

"Stop," he insisted. With his knuckles he tenderly brushed her cheek, pushed back strands of hair. "Being a parent isn't about bloodlines. It's all about love. There's no woman I know who's better at loving a child than you. Be my wife, Rachel. Be Heather's mother," he whispered. "Say yes. Let me love you."

In his eyes, smiling now, filled with love for her, Rachel saw the truth in his words. "Yes," she murmured before closing her eyes. He kissed her long and hard, and as they clung to each other, she memorized the moment, a keepsake of their beginning.

Epilogue

Dinner was pizza and wine in front of the television watching an old rerun. Rachel couldn't remember a more perfect evening. Sitting beside Kane on the sofa, she angled a quizzical look up at him. "When do you want to get married?"

He rested an arm on the back of the sofa behind her and skimmed his fingertips over the top of her arm. "Tomorrow."

Rachel rolled her eyes, drawing his laugh. "I'd like my sister and brother here," she said distractedly as sounds of Heather awakening came from the monitor on the coffee table. The monitor's counterpart was in Heather's bedroom. Reluctantly Rachel pushed herself to stand. "I should call them," she said while on her way to the kitchen for Heather's bottle.

He trailed her. "Okay."

On a laugh she turned and faced him.

Only inches behind her he held a hand out for the bottle. "Go ahead."

He'd changed. The loner, who'd kept himself isolated from others, had become a family man. Lovingly she touched his cheek, then gave the bottle to him. "I won't be long."

As he stood near the kitchen table, Rachel saw him run his fingers across the opened page of her mother's journal. "You stopped reading here?"

"Yes. I had something more important to do."

Looking back, he grinned. "See me?"

"Yes." She stepped closer as he absently turned a page. She watched a frown creep over his face. So much had changed since she'd first picked up the diary. "I'm hoping to find something that will tell me where Lenore went after she left Hubbard Bay."

He touched a corner of the book, turned it toward him. Rachel peered over his shoulder, read the passage he'd pointed to. "She's left town to have her child near relatives. Perhaps that's best. If she lived here, we'd want to see the baby."

"Look." He pointed to lines below those.

"Lenore called today from Arizona." Rachel frowned. "Arizona. Where in Arizona?"

Lightly he slipped a hand to the back of her neck and drew her face close. "We'll find out," he assured her.

In that moment, she knew she'd never have to face anything alone again. "I didn't think I wanted to know the person, but I did," she said, drawing back.

"What changed your mind?"

"Velma did. She made me see things more clearly." Rachel knew with acceptance in her heart that she couldn't rest now until they found the missing member of their family. "I have to call my brother and sister."

"Okay. I'll check on Heather." He kissed her brow, then stepped away.

It took only a few moments to relay everything to Sean, then Rachel called Gillian. "I learned that Lenore was living in Arizona before she had the baby."

"Alex Hunter lives in Arizona. Remember him?"

Her sister became friends with anyone and everyone. It was hard remembering all of them. But she'd remembered Alex. He was a professor. Muscular, intelligent, quite serious and Indiana-Jones gorgeous. He'd also been married then. "You were really good friends for a while and then went your separate ways."

"We reconnected after his divorce."

Rachel mentioned her conversation with Velma. "The relative could be the one who taught at the university. The sister. Edith."

"I wonder—Rachel, I might go to Arizona, search for all of them."

"Okay, if you want to."

"Don't you feel as if there's unfinished business here?"

Rachel had to admit that she was curious about Lenore, about finding the missing half sister or brother. Aware now of Gillian's sudden quietness again, Rachel asked the obvious. "Is there something you want to say?"

"I gather you've changed your mind about wanting to meet—"

"Dad's other child?" Rachel said unevenly. "Yes. It took a little time, but I finally realized what I was doing. How could I blame a child for what had happened?"

"Even if we don't find this person—" Gillian paused, then started again, "Well, we'll always have each other."

I have much more, Rachel mused. Nearby Kane glanced up from Heather. Cuddled in his arms, she closed her eyes, let the nipple slip from her mouth.

Rachel smiled at him. He'd given her something she'd never thought she'd find again—hope, faith in a future that held love and her own family. She moved near, the need to touch strong.

Looking up at her, he slid an arm around her waist. Rachel leaned over and kissed him with all the love in her heart. She had so much more than Gillian knew. She had a man who loved her and a beautiful baby girl. She had everything that she'd ever wanted.

*   *   *   *   *

*Read the continuation
of Jennifer Mikel's*
FAMILY REVELATIONS series with

HER HAND-PICKED FAMILY

(SE 1415) August 2001!

Beloved author
Sherryl Woods
is back with a brand-new miniseries

THE CALAMITY JANES

**Five women. Five Dreams.
A lifetime of friendship....**

On Sale May 2001—DO YOU TAKE THIS REBEL?
Silhouette Special Edition

On Sale August 2001—COURTING THE ENEMY
Silhouette Special Edition

On Sale September 2001—TO CATCH A THIEF
Silhouette Special Edition

On Sale October 2001—THE CALAMITY JANES
Silhouette Single Title

On Sale November 2001—WRANGLING THE REDHEAD
Silhouette Special Edition

"Sherryl Woods is an author who writes with
a very special warmth, wit, charm and intelligence."
—*New York Times* bestselling author
Heather Graham Pozzessere

Available at your favorite retail outlet.

Silhouette®
Where love comes alive™

Visit Silhouette at www.eHarlequin.com   SSETCJR

Feel like a star with Silhouette.

We will fly you and a guest to New York City for an
exciting weekend stay at a glamorous 5-star hotel.
Experience a refreshing day at one of New York's
trendiest spas and have your photo taken by a
professional. Plus, receive $1,000 U.S. spending money!

Flowers…long walks…dinner for two…
how does Silhouette Books
make romance come alive for you?

Send us a script, with 500 words or less, along with visuals (only drawings,
magazine cutouts or photographs or combination thereof). Show us how
Silhouette Makes Your Love Come Alive. Be creative and have fun. No
purchase necessary. All entries must be clearly marked with your name,
address and telephone number. All entries will become property of
Silhouette and are not returnable. **Contest closes September 28, 2001.**

Please send your entry to: **Silhouette Makes You a Star!**

In U.S.A.	In Canada
P.O. Box 9069	P.O. Box 637
Buffalo, NY, 14269-9069	Fort Erie, ON, L2A 5X3

Look for contest details on the next page, by visiting www.eHarlequin.com or
request a copy by sending a self-addressed envelope to the applicable address
above. Contest open to Canadian and U.S. residents who are 18 or over.
Void where prohibited.

Silhouette®
Where love comes alive™

Our lucky winner's photo will appear in a Silhouette ad. Join the fun!

HARLEQUIN "SILHOUETTE MAKES YOU A STAR!" CONTEST 1308
OFFICIAL RULES
NO PURCHASE NECESSARY TO ENTER

1. To enter, follow directions published in the offer to which you are responding. Contest begins June 1, 2001, and ends on September 28, 2001. Entries must be postmarked by September 28, 2001, and received by October 5, 2001. Enter by hand-printing (or typing) on an 8 ½" x 11" piece of paper your name, address (including zip code), contest number/name and attaching a script containing <u>500 words</u> or less, <u>along with drawings, photographs or magazine cutouts, or combinations thereof</u> (i.e., collage) <u>on no larger than 9" x 12"</u> piece of paper, describing how the <u>Silhouette books make romance come alive for you.</u> Mail via first-class mail to: Harlequin "Silhouette Makes You a Star!" Contest 1308, (in the U.S.) P.O. Box 9069, Buffalo, NY 14269-9069, (in Canada) P.O. Box 637, Fort Erie, Ontario, Canada L2A 5X3. Limit one entry per person, household or organization.

2. Contests will be judged by a panel of members of the Harlequin editorial, marketing and public relations staff. Fifty percent of criteria will be judged against script and fifty percent will be judged against drawing, photographs and/or magazine cutouts. Judging criteria will be based on the following:

   • Sincerity—25%
   • Originality and Creativity—50%
   • Emotionally Compelling—25%

   In the event of a tie, duplicate prizes will be awarded. Decisions of the judges are final.

3. All entries become the property of Torstar Corp. and may be used for future promotional purposes. Entries will not be returned. No responsibility is assumed for lost, late, illegible, incomplete, inaccurate, nondelivered or misdirected mail.

4. Contest open only to residents of the U.S. <u>(except Puerto Rico)</u> and Canada who are 18 years of age or older, and is void wherever prohibited by law; all applicable laws and regulations apply. Any litigation within the Province of Quebec respecting the conduct or organization of a publicity contest may be submitted to the Régie des alcools, des courses et des jeux for a ruling. Any litigation respecting the awarding of a prize may be submitted to the Régie des alcools, des courses et des jeux only for the purpose of helping the parties reach a settlement. Employees and immediate family members of Torstar Corp. and D. L. Blair, Inc., their affiliates, subsidiaries and all other agencies, entities and persons connected with the use, marketing or conduct of this contest are not eligible to enter. Taxes on prizes are the sole responsibility of the winner. Acceptance of any prize offered constitutes permission to use winner's name, photograph or other likeness for the purposes of advertising, trade and promotion on behalf of Torstar Corp., its affiliates and subsidiaries without further compensation to the winner, unless prohibited by law.

5. Winner will be determined no later than November 30, 2001, and will be notified by mail. Winner will be required to sign and return an Affidavit of Eligibility/Release of Liability/Publicity Release form within 15 days after winner notification. Noncompliance within that time period may result in disqualification and an alternative winner may be selected. All travelers must execute a Release of Liability prior to ticketing and must possess required travel documents (e.g., passport, photo ID) where applicable. Trip must be booked by December 31, 2001, and completed within one year of notification. No substitution of prize permitted by winner. Torstar Corp. and D. L. Blair, Inc., their parents, affiliates and subsidiaries are not responsible for errors in printing of contest, entries and/or game pieces. In the event of printing or other errors that may result in unintended prize values or duplication of prizes, all affected game pieces or entries shall be null and void. **Purchase or acceptance of a product offer does not improve your chances of winning.**

6. Prizes: (1) Grand Prize—A 2-night/3-day trip for two (2) to New York City, including round-trip coach air transportation nearest winner's home and hotel accommodations (double occupancy) at The Plaza Hotel, a glamorous afternoon makeover at <u>a trendy New York spa</u>, $1,000 in U.S. spending money and an opportunity to <u>have a professional photo taken and appear in a Silhouette advertisement</u> (approximate retail value: $7,000). (10) Ten Runner-Up Prizes of gift packages (retail value $50 ea.). Prizes consist of only those items listed as part of the prize. Limit one prize per person. Prize is valued in U.S. currency.

7. For the name of the winner (available after December 31, 2001) send a self-addressed, stamped envelope to: Harlequin "Silhouette Makes You a Star!" Contest 1197 Winners, P.O. Box 4200 Blair, NE 68009-4200 or you may access the www.eHarlequin.com Web site through February 28, 2002.

Contest sponsored by Torstar Corp., P.O Box 9042, Buffalo, NY 14269-9042.

If you enjoyed what you just read,
then we've got an offer you can't resist!

Take 2 bestselling love stories FREE!

Plus get a FREE surprise gift!

Clip this page and mail it to Silhouette Reader Service™

IN U.S.A.	IN CANADA
3010 Walden Ave.	P.O. Box 609
P.O. Box 1867	Fort Erie, Ontario
Buffalo, N.Y. 14240-1867	L2A 5X3

YES! Please send me 2 free Silhouette Special Edition® novels and my free surprise gift. After receiving them, if I don't wish to receive anymore, I can return the shipping statement marked cancel. If I don't cancel, I will receive 6 brand-new novels every month, before they're available in stores! In the U.S.A., bill me at the bargain price of $3.80 plus 25¢ shipping and handling per book and applicable sales tax, if any*. In Canada, bill me at the bargain price of $4.21 plus 25¢ shipping and handling per book and applicable taxes**. That's the complete price and a savings of at least 10% off the cover prices—what a great deal! I understand that accepting the 2 free books and gift places me under no obligation ever to buy any books. I can always return a shipment and cancel at any time. Even if I never buy another book from Silhouette, the 2 free books and gift are mine to keep forever.

235 SEN DFNN
335 SEN DFNP

Name	(PLEASE PRINT)	
Address	Apt.#	
City	State/Prov.	Zip/Postal Code

* Terms and prices subject to change without notice. Sales tax applicable in N.Y.
** Canadian residents will be charged applicable provincial taxes and GST.
  All orders subject to approval. Offer limited to one per household and not valid to
  current Silhouette Special Edition® subscribers.
  ® are registered trademarks of Harlequin Enterprises Limited.

SPED01   ©1998 Harlequin Enterprises Limited

SECRETS

A kidnapped baby
A hidden identity
A man with a past

Christine Rimmer's popular *Conveniently Yours*
miniseries returns with three brand-new books,
revolving around the Marsh baby kidnapped over
thirty years ago. Beginning late summer,
from Silhouette Books...

THE MARRIAGE AGREEMENT
(August 2001; Silhouette Special Edition #1412)
The halfbrother's story

THE BRAVO BILLIONAIRE
(September 2001; Silhouette Single Title)
The brother's story

THE MARRIAGE CONSPIRACY
(October 2001; Silhouette Special Edition #1423)
The missing baby's story—
all grown up and quite a man!

You won't want to miss a single one....
Available wherever Silhouette books are sold.

Where love comes alive™